The Clue of the Two Straws (annotated)

by G. H. Teed

Illustrated by Kenneth Brookes

Edited by Doug Frizzle

First published in the Union Jack magazine,
No. 1202, new series, 30 Oct. 1926

Stillwoods Edition

Stillwoods.Blogspot.Ca

Catalogue Information:
Title: The Clue of the Two Straws (annotated)
Author: G. H. Teed (1886-1938)
Illustrated by Kenneth Brookes
Edited by Doug Frizzle
First published in the Union Jack magazine, No. 1202, new series, 30 Oct. 1926
This Edition by: Stillwoods, 2024
ISBN Canada: 978-1-998819-39-3
Blog: Stillwoods.Blogspot.Ca
Author Blog: http://ghteed.blogspot.com/
Storefront: http://www.lulu.com/spotlight/lulubook22

Keywords: Nirvana, Yvonne Cartier, London, France, Europe

Sexton Blake and Yvonne; Tinker and Nirvana! What better quartette of favourites could "U.J." readers ask for in one story? What better quartette could the newcomer hope to meet? This yarn of thrills and action and fascinating detective work is a fitting setting for them, too.

https://tinyurl.com/ve25d42s This link should go to a spreadsheet of all known Teed stories. The list is annotated with various information on the stories and my progress with recapturing the work. The library of Teed's stories increases almost weekly. Check at Lulu.Com for the publications. Search for (space)Teed. /drf

Cautionary Note: This series of books by Stillwoods is intended to make the stories of G. H. Teed, born in New Brunswick, Canada, available to collectors and researchers. The editor, or rather digitizer has not altered the original publication.

This story may contain language and racial terms that are not appropriate today. I apologize for them; I know that the author was using his voice to excite and entertain an adventurous English audience. These works were published from 82 to 110 years ago. Most every work has characters of redeeming ethnicity within.

I hope you enjoy and share these stories; I have.

Doug Frizzle

Introduction to the Annotated Edition

- Facsimile Reproduction
- Supplementary Information
- Historical Context
- Collectors' Commentary
- Author Biographical Notes

This Stillwoods collection is about the author G. H. Teed. The great majority of his 500+ stories were written anonymously. They also, at the time, were issued under copyright —under the Sexton Blake banner. Teed wrote from 1913 until his death at the end of 1938. Since most of these works were anonymous, no-one knew he was a Canadian —or at least I have never seen a mention.

Teed's novels appeared in 'pulps' mostly —magazines with cheap paper, and issued mostly on a weekly basis. In original format, they are difficult to obtain today in undamaged condition. And they can be expensive!

Included in the ancillary material is the usual advertising for the next weekly issue.

Digitized by Doug Frizzle. This story may have also been digitized by others. Often those copies revise offensive terminology; I have retained the original terms only to indicate acceptable language of the day. Again I apologize to anyone that might be offended.

THE UNION JACK 1,198 · The Mystery of Room No. 7 · Anon. (G. H. Teed)

THE UNION JACK 1,199 · The Case of the Sheffield Ironmaster · Anon. (G. H. Teed)

THE UNION JACK 1,200 · The Affair of the Derelict Grange · Anon. (G. H. Teed)

THE UNION JACK 1,201 · The Mystery of the Venetian Palace · Anon. (G. H. Teed)

THE UNION JACK 1,202 · **The Clue of the Two Straws** · Anon. (G. H. Teed)

THE UNION JACK 1,203 · A Mystery of the Mountains · Anon.
(G. H. Teed)

These six stories, a hexalogy, appear to make an important
Yvonne and Nirvana series which was very popular. Although UJ
readers were unaware of the authors of the various Blake stories,
Teed's stories were quietly very popular with regular readers.

G. H. Teed spent a considerable time living in Europe after
WW1, probably due to his indebtedness which had been recognized in
England.

Contains some offensive racial terminology.

The PORCUPINE of PARIS!
(See the story of Lacombe, the Spiked Apache, on page 247.)

Eight pages of the 28 page magazine were missing from this
scan. So sorry . . . /drf

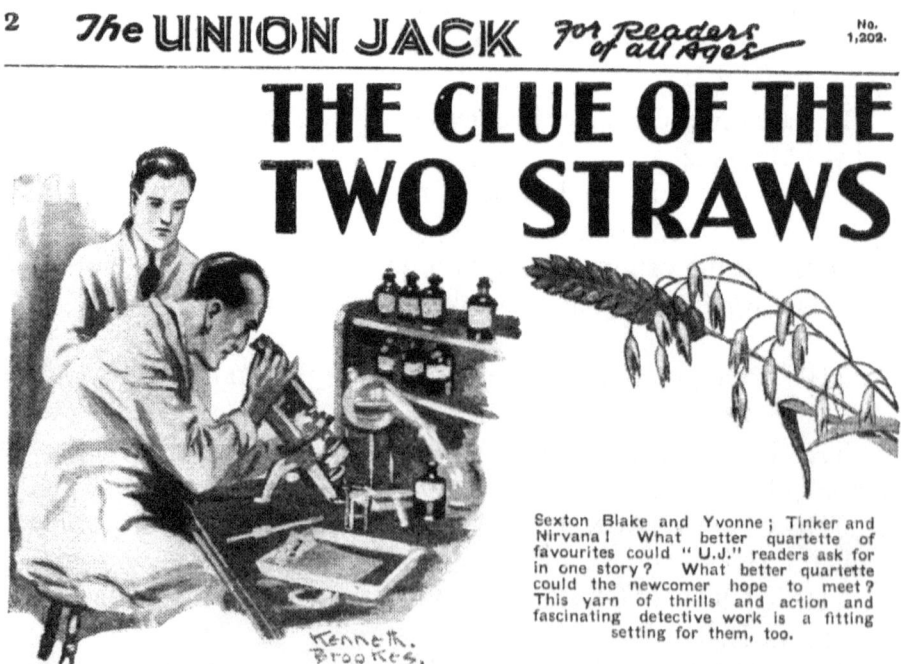

2 *The* UNION JACK *For Readers of all Ages* No. 1,202.

THE CLUE OF THE TWO STRAWS

Sexton Blake and Yvonne; Tinker and
Nirvana! What better quartette of
favourites could " U.J." readers ask for
in one story? What better quartette
could the newcomer hope to meet?
This yarn of thrills and action and
fascinating detective work is a fitting
setting for them, too.

Kenneth. Brookes.

THE FIRST CHAPTER

Yvonne Declares War.

"AND now, mademoiselle, perhaps you will do me the honour to enlighten me on the important matter you spoke of in your note? I am neither vain nor egotistical enough to believe that it was any personal attribute of mine that inspired you to suggest that I should meet you for tea at the Venetia."

Augustus Keever smiled quizzically at Yvonne as he held out his gold cigarette-case.

Yvonne abstracted a tube of choice Russian tobacco —wondering inwardly if Keever had discovered in some way that this was her pet brand —and studied him enigmatically while he held a gold lighter to the tip of the cigarette.

He had just said that he possessed no personal attractions which might make him a desirable companion. Yvonne was forced to admit to herself, however, that in a quite impersonal way he had a great deal to make him attractive to most women.

He was decidedly handsome in a restrained, distinguished manner; he was excellently dressed, and his manners of speech and person were beyond reproach.

And yet the man before her —well-bred, rich even as riches are accounted in these days, one of the ablest financiers in London, and a power in every money-market of Europe —was, with all these things to make life worth while, a scheming crook.

There must undoubtedly be a distinct kink somewhere in the man's brain, thought Yvonne, to make him risk all he had won for the certain disaster of criminal ways.

Until definite suspicion had been roused —until Sexton Blake had probed the many-ringed stockade which Keever had erected about his doings —there had been no cloud on the horizon.

And it had only been quite recently that Blake had been able to crystallise a suspicion he had held for a considerable time —that Augustus Keever was not the be-all and end-all of his gigantic intrigues, that even more powerful than he was "someone else" higher up —the person who had been vaguely referred to by the Paris police as the "mysterious monseigneur" and whom Blake had actually identified as Prince von Wadstein, a German scientist. [1]

Something of all this was passing through Yvonne's mind as she studied the faintly mocking eyes of the financier. It was quite true that she had written to him, asking him to take her to tea at the Venetia; it was true, too, that she had said that there was something of an important nature she had to speak of.

"You are right," she said slowly. "I did ask you to tea here in order to talk to you. And I propose being quite frank, Mr. Keever."

"I am glad, Miss Cartier. Anything else would not fit in with what I have heard of you."

"I shall not pretend to misunderstand you, Mr. Keever. I dare say you will hear lots about me and my so-called exploits if you care to take the trouble to inquire. But to our subject, I have asked you to meet me to-day to talk about Nirvana."

"I knew that."

"Very well. And now for a frank question. Why have you joined forces with those who persecute her, have persecuted her ever since she was a child? Surely a man of your substance and breeding can have little in common with persons like him who is known as Philippe the Fox and the woman, Marie?"

"In common, no; but they serve my purpose, mademoiselle," murmured Keever.

"I am not going to speak of your doings, except in so far as they affect Nirvana. Your affairs are your own, Mr. Keever. I shall not pretend to be ignorant of some of your doings, for little Nirvana has made me her confidant, and the way in which you permitted her to be treated in Venice was abominable. It is not going to happen again, Mr. Keever."

"It would be useless for me to protest that I was quite helpless to prevent what happened at Venice," he said after a pause.

Yvonne's deep, blue eyes grew scornful.

"In those words you acknowledge yourself to be at the beck and call of another, Mr. Keever. You ought to be above that. You ought to be the sort of man to stand on your own feet. But what you choose to do —with whom you elect to attach yourself —concerns me not.

"I want some sort of undertaking I can depend on that Nirvana is to be left alone in future. You may be helpless to combat the will of

---

1   For a fuller account as to Prince von Wadstein, see last week's issue: "The Mystery of the Venetian Palace " —Ed.

someone whose name I need not mention; but the woman Marie and Philippe the Fox are under your orders. If you say to them, 'Hands off Nirvana!' they will obey you. And it was cruel, unworthy of a man who professes to be what you have claimed, to get Nirvana into your power by promising her something you knew you could not give her. You know that her greatest desire in life is to find her father. You pledged your word to take her to him, when you knew no more than I where he was to be found."

Keever flushed a little under the lash of Yvonne's scorn. What she said was all true enough, and Keever could not deny it. He made as if to speak, but before he could do so Yvonne went on:

"And to all that you added the excuse that you wanted her near you because you loved her. A pretty way of showing love, Mr. Keever! If you had cared for her at all it would have been your one aim to keep her away from all association with people like Marie and her like."

"You may find it difficult to understand, but I would have done anything for her," he returned, his voice vibrating with emotion. "I had nothing but suffering when she suffered."

"Then you should have risen above selfishness. But if you mean one part of what you say, then you will give me the promise which I have asked. You say you have heard something of me, Mr. Keever. For some time past it has pleased me to live quietly. But there are certain circumstances that would cause me to take a very active part in things.

"I am not altogether without brains and resources, Mr. Keever. And I tell you now that if I do not get an assurance from you that I can depend on I am going to take a very active part in Nirvana's affairs. I am not unprovided with ammunition with which to open the campaign."

Keever frowned. He had not been at all disinclined to meet the charming Mademoiselle Yvonne, for he had indeed heard much of her, and he wanted to weigh up at close quarters the person who was championing Nirvana. But he had not the faintest intention of giving the promise which she demanded.

Things were approaching a crisis with Augustus Keever; but outwardly, in the City and elsewhere, there was not the faintest sign of this.

But Keever knew that from the moment Sexton Blake had

3

identified him in connection with the mysterious monseigneur he had been marked down. It wasn't only a case of he must "get" Blake first, or Blake would "get" him. He intended to settle Sexton Blake the first opportunity that offered.

But eliminating Blake would not remove the danger. It could, at best, only postpone the inevitable. Scotland Yard and the Paris Surete had been kept too well posted by Blake.

And he did not make the mistake of underestimating the enmity of Mademoiselle Yvonne. He was far from anxious to have her as an additional enemy, and yet he could not bring himself to give up hope of Nirvana. Augustus Keever had been thinking for some time past that if things came to the worst he would clear out. He had salted away a hoard sufficient to make him a rich man in some country where the extradition laws were not operative. And, when he went, he intended that Nirvana should go with him.

Moreover, while one statement of Yvonne's would have been quite correct a short time before, it was not so on that October afternoon when they sat in one corner of the Venetia lounge watching the dancers and discussing the fate of Nirvana.

When he had promised Nirvana to take her to her father he had been making a promise he could not fulfil. But now he did know the whereabouts of her father. It had taken him many months and the expenditure of much money to solve that mystery; but he had succeeded, and, with this actual bait, he had no intention of relinquishing Nirvana.

Hence his frown. Men were not few who would have found it easy to say "yes" to anything proposed by the lovely girl who sat opposite Keever, but the financier, even if Nirvana had not occupied his thoughts to the entire exclusion of anyone else of her sex, would not have trod that path.

He had sense enough to know that he could never carry the citadel of Yvonne's heart by any assault he might attempt. He had heard things from time to time —whispers and hints of Yvonne's name being linked with that of Sexton Blake. It had meant nothing to him at the time.

To-day, however, he was wondering if Yvonne was acting only on her own initiative or whether Blake was in the background. If Sexton Blake was interested, it could only be on Tinker's account. And that thought was to Augustus Keever like the proverbial red rag to a bull. It seemed almost ludicrous that a man of his years could be jealous of a lad Tinker's age, but there it was.

At last he gave Yvonne her answer.

"You want a direct 'yes' or 'no,' and I will give it to you, Miss Cartier. It is 'no'—most emphatically so! And if it is of any interest to you, I can tell you, without any prevarication, that what I did not possess before I have in my possession to-day. I do know where Nirvana's father is to be found."

Yvonne's wits were working fast. But her voice was casual enough as she said:

"I am sorry that is your decision, Mr. Keever. But I warn you here and now that Nirvana's battle is mine. I shall do everything in my power to thwart your purpose, while she is under my protection. And since there is nothing to be gained by prolonging an interview that can only be unpleasant to both of us, I shall be glad if you will put me into a taxi."

"Then it is to be war," remarked Keever, as he stood waiting while Yvonne drew on her gloves.

She nodded briefly. Anyone observing them in the fashionable lounge at that moment would never have dreamed that a keen battle of wits was in progress between the well-groomed pair. Their manner was as light and inconsequential as if they were talking of the merest trifles.

"It is war —to the end," he heard her say in a low tone. Her wonderful eyes held his for the fraction of a minute, and then, with the slightest possible shrug, she made her way along the side of the room.

When he had put her into a taxi, Augustus Keever called another and drove through to his house just off Eaton Place. It was just as the cab drew away from the kerb in front of the Venetia that he looked out of the window to find himself gazing straight into the eyes of the young fellow who was most in his thoughts at that moment.

Tinker, Sexton Blake's assistant, had been walking down Piccadilly when he happened to see Keever assisting Yvonne into a taxi, and the sight puzzled him for, from all appearances, the two appeared on the most friendly terms. Therefore, when he caught Keever's glance, he was frowning heavily, and the financier, guessing the reason, smiled superciliously, thereby adding to Tinker's acute desire to throttle him.

5

But, once on his way to Eaton Place, Augustus Keever lost his smile.

He was sensible enough to realise that he had by no means added to his chances by deliberately seeking the enmity of Mademoiselle Yvonne. He was no fool, and he did not make the mistake of underestimating her capacity for mischief. He wanted to be alone in his study and think.

He had some very tricky business afoot just then which would stand a good chance of being wrecked completely if even a breath of suspicion were wafted against it. He wanted to go over every point once more and try, if possible, to put his finger on any weak point which might exist.

He had a feeling that instead of waiting for things to happen, Mademoiselle Yvonne might attack, and if she enlisted Sexton Blake under her banner, then it behoved him to keep a wary eye open.

His instinct there was true, but he little dreamed how Yvonne was going to open hostilities that very night.

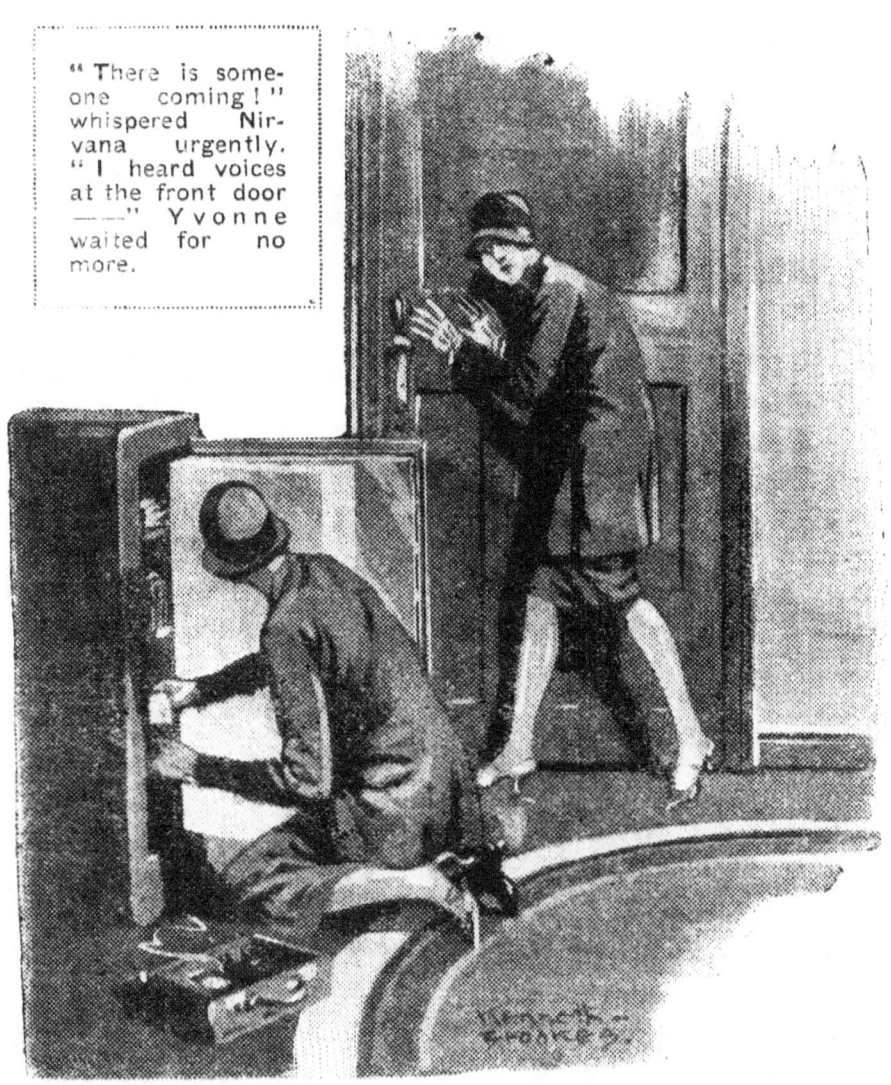

"There is some-one coming!" whispered Nirvana urgently. "I heard voices at the front door ———" Yvonne waited for no more.

THE SECOND CHAPTER.

While the Iron is Hot.

"SO that's that, my dear! It is at least something to know exactly where we stand with Augustus Keever."

Yvonne and Nirvana were sitting before a cosy fire in the smoking-room at the end of the hall in Yvonne's duplex flat at Queen Anne's Gate. It was about an hour since Yvonne had left the financier at the Venetia, and she had just finished telling the younger girl of her interview.

For the moment they had the flat to themselves, Graves, Yvonne's uncle, being still at his club, and Yvonne had little difficulty in guessing in what particular room in that classic rendezvous, for Graves was miserable when in town without his afternoon game of bridge.

So far, however, Yvonne had said nothing to Nirvana about Keever's statement that he had at last actually discovered the whereabouts of her father. Yvonne had not lost sight of the fact that he might only be lying again, and she did not want to make Nirvana miserable by raising hopes which she might find it impossible to bring to fruition.

Nirvana, clad in a blue silk boudoir wrap, slid from her chair on to the big, soft-cushioned stool at Yvonne's feet.

"Why do you take so much trouble about my poor affairs?" she asked softly. "You are too good to me, Yvonne. I know that Augustus Keever will not rest until he has me back in his power. He is like that, he never yields an inch. And, besides, there are Marie and Philippe the Fox to help him. Marie is the worst of all. She is furious that I am under your protection and out of her reach."

Yvonne stroked the golden head that rested against her knee.

"We shall certainly prove ourselves equal to Keever and any number of them, my dear. If the game gets too strenuous, we have strong allies of our own to call upon."

Nirvana's ear showed pink as she blushed, for she knew to whom Yvonne referred.

Suddenly the elder girl spoke again.

"Nirvana, when you were at Keever's house, did you see into

most of the rooms?"

"Yes. Until things got difficult, I had the run of the place, but I was not allowed to go out."

"I have seen it from the outside, but I wish you would tell me how the interior is arranged. It does not look very large."

"It isn't. It is quite small, but very well furnished. He has spent a great deal of money on it, I should think. There isn't any drawing-room in the ordinary sense of the term. In front on the ground floor there is a big front-room which he has made a dining-room. Then at the end of the hall is a study in which he used to spend most of his time. Then what used to be the dining-room has been made into a sort of smoking lounge where he receives most of his visitors. Only his intimate friends are taken into the study."

"I see. And on the upper floors?"

"The first floor is given over entirely to his private apartments. I have never been in the rooms there. The next floor contains three rooms and a bath-room. One of the rooms is a sitting-room, and it was in a suite there that I was kept prisoner. The upper floor is used by servants —or rather the cook and her husband. Caesar, the black personal servant, of whom I told you, sleeps in the basement, and the other servants, a woman and a boy, come in by the day."

"I understand. Now, about his study —have you any idea if he transacts much business there?"

"I do not know for certain, but I should think so. There were always lots of people coming and going."

"Have you observed the safe? I suppose there is one?"

"Yes. It is a large affair, very modern, I should say, and it looked very strong."

"Looks are not everything in a safe," murmured Yvonne. "I shall be able to tell better when I have seen it."

Nirvana looked up sharply.

"Seen it, Yvonne? How shall you manage that? You are not going to see him again, are you?"

Yvonne smiled and reached for the cigarettes. When she had taken a few puffs she looked down at Nirvana.

"What an alarmed little mouse it is," she said lightly. "Yes, despite your fears, I am going to make a call upon Augustus Keever, dear. And I think I shall go this evening."

"But why, Yvonne? It is dangerous for you to go there, and you must not do so. If you insist, then you must let me go, too. Keever is a dangerous man who will stop at nothing. If you deliberately put yourself in his power, you won't find it easy to get away. I know, for I have experienced it."

"The cases are not parallel, dear. Besides, I shall go prepared for anything Mr. Keever might do. As a matter of fact, I should much prefer that he wasn't in the house when I go. But if he is, then I shall have to chance it,"

Nirvana wrinkled her brows.

"You have some plan, Yvonne. But what is it, please? You must not embark on something for me without telling me what it is. And if you go there, I insist that you let me come, too."

"I think I shall, Nirvana, we shall see. What I propose doing is to try and have a look inside the safe in the study there. As I am quite certain Mr. Keever would not reveal its contents at our request, it is necessary that we should view them without his knowledge. If he should be out this evening, I have an idea that might be all right. On the other hand, if he doesn't go out then our visit will have to be postponed until a later hour. But by hook or by crook I am going to strike while the iron is hot, and make an effort to open that safe to-night."

"But what does it contain that you want, Yvonne? It must be something awfully important to make you take such risks."

"You'll know soon enough, kitten, if it is there. And, after all, I think you may come with me."

"But, of course, that has been my intention all along."

Yvonne laughed and rose. "Explanations to uncle might be awkward, so I think I shall telephone him at his club, and tell him he must dine there to-night. By the way, Nirvana, had Augustus Keever any regular time for going out in the evening —that is, when he dined at home?"

"I don't know that, Yvonne."

"Well, never mind. I shall have Alec put an inquiry through at nine o'clock. If he is going out, he will be gone by then; if not, we shall have to pay the gentleman a visit after he has retired."

AT nine o'clock, in obedience to Yvonne's instructions, Alec, the chauffeur, telephoned to Augustus Keever's house from the garage at the back of the mansions. At ten minutes past nine he was at the door of Yvonne's flat to make his report.

"Some voice that sounded like a coon's answered, and said that Mr. Keever had gone out, miss. I asked what time he was expected back, and he said he didn't know. Wanted to know if there was a message for his master, and I said it didn't matter."

"Quite right, Alec. And now get the saloon ready to go out. Bring it round at half-past ten sharp."

"Very good, Miss Yvonne."

"We shall leave presently," said Yvonne to Nirvana when she was back in the smoking-room. "I think you had better get out of that frock and put on a dark costume. I shall do the same."

"Is he at home now?"

"No; and a voice that Alec says sounded like that of a negro informed him that he did not know what time he would return. I suppose it must have been the negro, Caesar."

"Probably. But the negro will be there if we go now, Yvonne."

"I know; but I don't anticipate much trouble handling him. Bring your small pistol, if you wish, dear; but I don't think you will find much use for it."

Despite the advice she had given Nirvana, Yvonne made her own preparations with utmost care. She changed her light dinner-frock for a dark blue costume, and drew on a cloche hat that came well down over her eyes. In a capacious leather handbag she placed several articles, among which were a small bottle containing a colourless liquid, a soft flannel pad; an automatic pistol, a miniature but very effective microphone, some thin keys, an electric torch, and a small, shining steel instrument which had been invented by Sexton Blake, and was, without exception, the most efficient little tool to be found for the persuasion of a reluctant lock. Tinker had christened it the "spider." There were one or two other items but the above made up the most important.

When she was ready she descended to the smoking-room, where she found Nirvana waiting. The younger girl had also donned a blue coat and skirt, and carried a handbag, into which she had thrust not only a pistol, but other things as well. When it came to the prospect of danger Nirvana was not lacking in nerve.

At exactly half-past ten Yvonne led the way out, and found, as she expected, the big saloon car standing at the kerb. She gave Alec brief instructions, and got in after Nirvana. Alec drove round by way of Victoria Street, and, branching off there opposite the Grosvenor Hotel, continued on to Eaton Place. He turned into the street where Keever's house was situated, but did not go on as far as that. He drew up some thirty or forty yards away, and there Yvonne and Nirvana got out.

"Wait round the corner in the square," said Yvonne. "I can't tell how long we shall be, but remain there until we come. And be ready to get away at once. When we come we may come running."

"Very good, Miss Yvonne. I'll have everything ready to go on the jump. But I'd like to lend a hand, if I may."

Yvonne shook her head. Not that Alec would not have been of value. The faithful fellow, like everyone else in her employ, had taken part in many an affair of hers, and would have gone the limit at a word from his beloved mistress. But this was not an occasion when Yvonne expected any strong arm work would be necessary. As she figured things, they had only Caesar, the negro butler, to deal with, and she had a plan ready for that emergency. Therefore she wanted Alec to be where she could find him quickly, if things went wrong.

"You can be most useful out here, Alec. Don't get nervous if we are gone some time. What I have to do in that house may prove difficult."

With that she touched Nirvana's arm, and the two girls walked along to the house, while the saloon drifted back into the square. There was a light to be seen over the fanlight of the door, but the narrow street appeared to be empty save for themselves.

It was only a short thoroughfare, with scarcely more than a dozen houses in it, ending in a dead wall which was the back of other houses in a street beyond. It carried little foot, or wheeled traffic at any time, and this evening, with a drizzle setting in, conditions could not have been better.

Yvonne led the way up the steps, and paused for a few moments before pressing the bell. Over the area railings they could see a light in the basement.

"The cook and her husband," whispered Yvonne. "You said they usually retired about ten?"

"Yes."

"It is now about a quarter to eleven. Do you think it possible they can still be up?"

"No; Caesar sits down there when he is waiting up."

"All right. We will have to chance it. Now get ready to put something over your face. I have brought two masks, which I have fixed up with luminous paste. I have made them as terrifying as I could. We will give Caesar a shock, and that will give me time for the other thing I have to do."

Yvonne took out the two masks which she had made ready, and as she unfolded one, a ghastly set of features shone out. It was made as grotesque as some terrifying gargoyle, and when Nirvana had donned it, she was certainly a fearsome sight. Yvonne arranged the second, equally as horrible, over her own features, and then her hands were busy for a few moments inside the bag. When she finally withdrew them, she whispered:

"Now the bell, Nirvana, and when the man comes, leave him to me."

Nirvana pressed the button, and the two stood waiting. Presently they heard the sound of footsteps coming along the hall, and next followed the click of the spring catch as the knob was turned. Then the door swung open, revealing Caesar's black countenance.

For a moment he stood goggling at the two terrifying goblins that stared at him from the gloom, the whites of his eyes showing wide in sudden terror.

"Lawdy —lawdy me!" he gasped. "All's done! Oh, mah lawdy! Ah —my —"

But that was as far as he got. Up underneath his paralysed arm came a gloved hand; against his gaping mouth and wide nostrils went a pad saturated with chloroform, and as he fell back gasping, Yvonne followed, keeping up the pressure of the pad. A few seconds only, and then Caesar slid to the floor at her feet.

Yvonne replaced the pad in her bag and motioned to Nirvana to close the door. Then she took out a large silk gag of the "pear" variety —the most efficient and at the same time most uncomfortable, for the reason that, once it is behind the teeth, the silk bulge expands to the full capacity of the mouth —and some thin but very strong silk cord.

Nirvana lent a hand, and in a few minutes Caesar was trussed up soundly. It was no easy matter for the two girls to drag the heavy black along the hall and down the stairs to the basement, but they managed it, and at last they stood in the study, the lights on, Nirvana at the door listening, and Yvonne's eyes resting on the black enamelled front and the glittering nickel combination of the big safe which stood in one corner. So far things had gone absolutely according to plan.

Now Yvonne moved with swift precision. Once again the capacious handbag was brought into use. and on the rug in front of the safe. Yvonne laid out a few nickel-plated instruments she had brought, together with the microphone.

This latter was equipped with two small rubber suction cones, by which it could be quickly attached to the door of the safe just under the knob of the combination, the system being of the American type by which the tumblers were controlled by a series of points on the numbered dial, so many turns to the right for one, so many to the left for another, and so on until the tumblers fell.

It was a far more difficult sort than the old-fashioned lettered type, but Yvonne had made an exhaustive study of every kind of lock combination, and there were few that would not yield to her persuasive touch.

It took only a couple of seconds to get the microphone into place, then, bending down so that one pink ear was close to the little instrument, she began to twist the polished knob first in one direction, then in another.

Nirvana watched her from the doorway where she stood on guard, fascinated at the cool certainty with which Yvonne went to work. It seemed amazing to Nirvana that a girl who possessed every feminine attribute in such superlative degree as did Yvonne, could tackle a complicated safe under such conditions with nerves rock-steady, and manner quite unhurried.

Yvonne's profile was towards her, and now and then the red, shapely lips would give a little move of satisfaction which told the other that things were progressing. As a matter of fact, there was not the tiniest click within that complicated arrangement of slides and tumblers that was not magnified by the microphone, so that Yvonne could hear it, and read its meaning.

There was an unmistakable fall which told her when the first action of the tumblers had taken place, and not long after that she succeeded in getting the second fall. If took longer to bring the third twist of the combination into action, but, when she heard the tell-tale noise once more, she lifted her head and tried to turn the handle.

It refused to yield, proof that it was something more than a triple arrangement she had to solve; so she laid her ear once more against the microphone and began twisting the knob once more to the left. One complete circle of the indicator did she make without getting the slightest response from within a second effort produced the same absence of result; a third left the soulless metal as unresponsive as ever; but a fourth brought that unmistakable click that told her she was probing its secret.

And this time, when she tried the handle, it yielded to her pressure.

But she was not through yet, for as she swung the heavy door open, she saw herself confronted by a polished oak inner door which was fitted with an upper and lower lock.

That, however, was comparatively simple to manage. It was the little instrument which Tinker had christened a "spider" that Yvonne now brought into play. Into one of the keyholes she insinuated one of the tips of the spider —it looked far more like a crab —and then began working this flexible bit of ring-covered wire in and out until it gradually assumed the exact cutting of the lock within. When it would yield no longer to her pressure, she closed her hand over the body of the spider, and turned ever so gently.

Click!

The lock turned as easily as if she had fitted the proper key. She made the same swift work of the upper lock, and once more swung wide the barricade which lay before her, and the object of her search.

Now the interior of the safe lay exposed to her view. The lower half was divided into several narrow vertical compartments which were full of private account books of various sorts. These Yvonne ignored, turning her attention to the compartments in the upper half, some of which were horizontal and some vertical. And, in the centre of the upper half was a small steel door forming a sort of safe within a safe. Beneath this again were two shallow drawers fitted with polished brass locks.

The open compartments yielded several bundles of documents that appeared, even at a cursory glance, as if they might prove interesting reading. But Yvonne had come seeking a certain thing, and she did not allow these to distract her from her object.

She soon assured herself that what she was looking for was not among these papers, so she replaced them and turned her attention to the small steel door. It was not fitted with a combination, but one look at the narrow, indented slit of the lock told Yvonne it was going to be no easy matter to force it.

As a matter of fact it called into play the very smallest of the flexible "claws" of the spider, and even this only went in under the most gentle persuasion. If ever she needed delicacy of touch, it was just then.

With a perfection of judgment and a precision of touch that would have evoked the admiration of the cunningest safe breaker, she manipulated that thin bit of flexible steel until it was almost entirely lost from view. Then she began to turn and twist with the lightest pressure imaginable.

It did not fail her. When she knew that any more pressure would only bend the delicate thread of metal beyond further use, she laid her fingers on the small steel knob above the lock. She drew it towards her gently and then a little sigh of satisfaction escaped her as it came open.

She did not even glance at the interior until she had made sure that the spider was hanging in such a way that it would not fall out; but then her eager gaze probed into the farthest reaches of the shadowy corners. At first she seemed to see nothing but several packets of folded papers, the coloured blending of green and gold proclaiming that they were share or bond certificates of some sort.

Yvonne took hold of some of the topmost bundles and was about to draw them out when a long, thin blue envelope, which she had not noticed before, slid off and fell against her bent knee.

She picked it up, and saw that it was carefully sealed with heavy red sealing-wax. The impress was a complicated arrangement, which she took to be Keever's crest. On turning it over, she found that just one word, or part of a word, had been written on it in red ink. And as she saw what those letters were her tongue clicked very softly. To be exact, there were only four, but these were:

"Nirv."

If that contraction didn't stand for Nirvana, then Yvonne couldn't think what it could mean. And the care with which the thin enclosure had been sealed proved that Augustus Keever set no small store by it —that fact and its inclusion among the valuable certificates in the inner strong box.

Yvonne dropped the envelope into her bag, and again picked up one of the bundles of certificates. She slipped one out, and, unfolding it, had just time to see that it was a bearer bond belonging to a post-war reconstruction issue of a central European country, value £100, when her attention was caught by a low, warning hiss from Nirvana. She looked up quickly, to find the other coming across the room towards her.

"There is someone coming," she whispered urgently. "I am sure I heard voices at the front door and the sound of a bell somewhere."

Yvonne waited for no more. Almost mechanically she swept several bundles of the bonds into her bag and closed the door of the inner safe. She worked swiftly, with a steady hand, turning the upper lock, but not daring to risk the time on the lower one. Next she closed the wooden door, leaving it on its ordinary catch. When the big steel door had been pushed in and the nickelled knob given a twirl the combination closed automatically.

Then, even as she came to her feet, Yvonne gathered up her few instruments and made for the door, where Nirvana was again listening.

One moment she kept her ear pressed against it until she heard voices close at hand, and the tread of feet, as they came towards the study. Then she switched out the light, and, catching Nirvana by the hand, drew her along towards the heavy velvet curtains which she had noticed hung over the window embrasure.

Scarcely had they reached their shelter when the door of the study was flung open!

THE THIRD CHAPTER.

Touch and Go.

FROM the noise and different voices it was plain that several persons had entered. Yvonne had no difficulty in recognising Augustus Keever's tones, and she also made out the lighter timbre of a woman's voice. But it was when Nirvana pressed her lips close to her ear that Yvonne knew.

"It is Marie," Nirvana breathed, "and Philippe the Fox."

Yvonne pressed her arm to let her know that she understood, and to warn her to be careful; then the two girls stood, scarcely breathing, while the chairs were run across the floor and there followed the unmistakable signs of a general settling.

Followed the sound of liquid being poured into glasses, low-voiced inquiries from Keever. monosyllabic answers from Marie and the Fox, the fizzing sound of soda, the tinkle of glass again, and then: "Well, I'm glad I found you two at home. I brought another two hundred thousand home to-day, and you will have to get busy to-morrow selling them. Better handle a hundred thousand each, as before. That will bring the total up to exactly two millions. And at that we will have completed the job here, in England. I'll give you the bonds before you go."

Yvonne felt Nirvana's fingers clutch at her, but again she cautioned her with a pressure.

"What about brokers?" continued Keever, after a pause, during which the two girls could hear a throaty gurgle as one of the trio swallowed some of the drink. "I think it would be wise to pick out a new outfit each."

"I have already arranged my end of it," the listeners heard Marie drawl. "Just the same, I shall be glad when this last lot is disposed of. It has been a big flood to let loose on this market, and I feel uneasy about it. Something is going to slip one day, and I don't want to be underneath when it goes."

"Same here!" remarked the Fox.

"What's the matter?" sneered Keever. "Are you two getting cold feet? All you have to do is to sell some perfectly good bonds at market price —or they are near enough perfectly good bonds to pass as such. You have both had a big rake off, and ought to have salted away a nice bunch of money out of the deal.

"Look what I have had to do in the business! I have had to act as the London financial house for passing them on, and if anything slipped it is I who would run the greatest risk. But I don't think you will fall down on it after all that has gone. If you do," —here Keever paused— "I shouldn't like to be you when 'monseigneur' hears of it."

"Who said anything about falling down on it?" demanded Marie angrily. "A little less of that, Keever! We are not entirely in your power. We can make things just as hot for you as you can for us. There is quite a lot about that last affair in Venice that 'monseigneur' would like to know. If you open your mouth too wide we can do the same. We are partners in this business, not your servants, and don't you forget it!"

"What Marie says goes for me, too!" chimed in the Fox. "Walk a little more lightly, Keever, unless you want to stumble."

"You two must be suffering from nerves," said Keever evenly. "You, Marie, are as touchy as a stick of dynamite, and have been ever since we left Venice. I suppose you still blame me for letting Nirvana slip out of our hands?"

"Whose fault was it if it wasn't yours?"

"Your own, my dear girl. If you hadn't chosen the moment you did to let your fury loose, then monseigneur wouldn't have overheard, and, therefore, wouldn't have known that she was at the window signalling to that cub of Sexton Blake's when he passed along the canal. That was what upset everything, and it was not the fault of anyone here that the place was raided that same evening.

"But monseigneur feels very sore about that whole business, let me tell you. It is all very well for you to let yourself go here, but take my warning and lay very low when he is about.

"Let me impress upon you that in the game he is playing we are all of us just so many cogs. As for me, I am taking no chances. That is all I have to say, but if you don't curb that tongue and temper of yours you will find yourself in a very nasty place one of these days. And, despite the fact that Philippe echoes everything you say, he knows I am speaking wisdom."

"Well, Keever is right there!" grumbled the Fox.

"And now, while we are on the subject of Nirvana, let me tell you what happened to-day," went on Keever, after an appreciable silence.

"I wish you had been with me, Marie. I should like to have seen the two of you together."

"Two of whom? What are you talking about?"

"I had tea to day with Mademoiselle Yvonne."

If Keever had wished to startle Marie he succeeded, for the two eavesdroppers could hear her give a gasp, while the Fox swore audibly. Then Keever began, and gave what Yvonne was bound to acknowledge was an uncoloured version of their interview at the Venetia.

"So there is no more doubt in that quarter," he wound up. "It is war, and, from all I have heard, this person they call Mademoiselle Yvonne is not to be despised. You will have to watch your step, Marie."

"I ask for nothing better than to meet her," responded Marie. "There is a score between us that will be settled when the time comes. It is she who is keeping Nirvana away from us, and I'll see that she pays as well as Nirvana."

"And I'll help you there," said Keever harshly. "I'll pull every string you show me, Marie, to beat her at that game. If we don't get Nirvana back, things are going to get more and more complicated. This Mademoiselle Yvonne is hand-and-glove with Sexton Blake; Nirvana will talk, and that adds to our danger. Sexton Blake has got to be settled once and for all, but before then we must get Nirvana back.

"That is really what I wanted to see you about to-night. I intend to give every moment after to-morrow to try and devise a scheme, and I want both of you to help me. The moment you show me a successful plan, Marie, you can write yourself a cheque for any sum you like to name."

"I'd do it without that," she answered sharply. "I already have a plan; when it is ready to be put into effect I'll tell you. And now, what about those bonds? I think Philippe and I ought to be getting away soon."

"I'll get them."

As Keever's chair creaked Yvonne drew Nirvana close to her, and her lips moved close against the other's ear.

"He will find. Our only chance to take them by surprise. Keep close to me. Get pistol ready. Stick tight every second, and do just as I do!"

Nirvana pressed her arm to show she understood, and then they stood even more tensely than before, listening to the faint sounds at the safe as Keever worked the combination. They could hear the swish of the suction as the big door swung open; then, after a moment or so, came a low exclamation from Keever.

"That's funny!" they heard him say.

"What is it?" came in the Fox's smooth tones.

"This inner door is unlocked. Could have sworn I locked it. Never happened before. Can't understand, but everything seems all right."

The tinkle of a key followed now, and Keever must have attacked the upper lock of the small steel door first, for he made no remarks about it. But a little later, when Yvonne judged he must be trying to turn the lower lock, which was already thrust back, he again gave an exclamation of surprise.

Yvonne waited just about ten seconds after that. She strained forward until she heard the sound of the steel clang on being thrown back, then there came a sound which told her that Keever had discovered certain papers to be missing, and on that she acted.

In one sweep she threw aside the heavy curtains, her next movement carried her into the room before the astounded gaze of Philippe the Fox and Marie.

That pair were still held rigid, with Keever frozen on his knees in sheer astonishment, when Yvonne gained her third position of vantage by reaching the other side of the room close to the door.

Nirvana had kept close to her, and now, as the spell broke, the two girls threw up their pistols, Yvonne covering Marie and the Fox, while Nirvana held a steady barrel in a line with Augustus Keever's body.

Yvonne was human enough, and quite feminine enough even in the stress of the moment, to feel a strong desire to say a few things to Marie. The latter's words a few minutes before had not fallen on deaf ears. But, with the responsibility of Nirvana, Yvonne held herself in check. When she did speak her voice was as cool and impersonal and her words as clipped as Blake himself could have made them.

"Keep Mr. Keever covered. Nirvana. If he makes the slightest attempt to rise, shoot, and shoot low. As for you two," she added, speaking to Marie and the Fox, but keeping her eye on the former, "I assure you I shall not hesitate to press this trigger if you try to leave your chairs. I might add that this pistol is loaded, and I believe Mr.

Keever has already been good enough to say that I am not to be trifled with.

"I had not intended that we should be found here, but since the unforeseen has happened, it is, perhaps, just as well. It will give me the opportunity to say to you all that I stand by what I told Mr. Keever this afternoon. From now on I take an active interest in Nirvana's affairs. What is aimed at her is aimed at me as well. Just think that over, all three of you, and pass it on to your 'mysterious monseigneur' as well. I have an idea it might interest Prince von Wadstein. Now come, Nirvana!"

As she shot out the command Yvonne stepped forward, jerked open the door, and hustled Nirvana out into the hall. She slipped through after her, and not until then did any of the others realise that while she had been talking she had been working at the key with her free hand.

On the moment the door slammed Augustus Keever was up with an oath. Philippe the Fox was not a second behind, and Marie was no laggard. Outside the door Yvonne was trying desperately to get the key in, and turned, before the door could be torn open. She knew how slim their chances of escape were if they should have to run the gauntlet of the hall.

Nirvana, who was clinging on to the handle, felt it turn in her hand. She gave a gasp of warning to Yvonne, and still another as she thought the door was being drawn inwards. But just then Yvonne raised herself and caught Nirvana's arm.

"It's all right —I've locked it! Come on! The door will hold for a little!"

The two girls raced up the hall to the front door. Behind them a terrific assault was being made on the other portal. Yvonne remembered that there was a spring lock on the inside of the front door, and unless Keever had put the chain in place —which wasn't likely, since he had expected Marie and the Fox to leave soon —there should not be anything else in between them and freedom.

Nor was there. The knob turned easily enough, and both girls laughed a little hysterically as they felt the rush of cool, damp air against their faces.

Yvonne could not resist pausing to look back along the hall, and it was then, as they stood silhouetted in the opening, that the study door came open with a crash. Between them, Keever and the Fox had driven it off its hinges.

They waited for no more. Through the porch and down the steps they sped, then along to Eaton Place where Alec should be waiting. As they turned into the square they could see two figures racing after them. But Alec was standing by the saloon ready for instant action, and by the time Yvonne and Nirvana had tumbled in he was at the wheel "stepping on the gas."

They shot down one side of the square at reckless speed, and then round a corner almost on two wheels. Looking back, Yvonne caught a brief glimpse of two figures under a light —just a flash —then they were gone.

She sank back with a low laugh.

"A close shave, Nirvana dear, but we did it! And I am not so sure but I found more to-night in that safe of Augustus Keever's than I expected or hoped."

"What do you mean, Yvonne?" asked Nirvana, snuggling into her.

"Never mind now, child. I want to have a look at them first. Then, perhaps I will tell you."

And more than that Yvonne would not say just then.

THE FOURTH CHAPTER.

Carelessness or Crime?

MR. SEXTON BLAKE arrived in Lombard Street a few minutes after half past eleven in the morning and, leaving Tinker at the kerb in the Grey Panther, entered the big stone building which, among other financial firms, housed the stockbroking concern of Harborough & Whittaker. It was James Whittaker, the junior partner, who had telephoned to Blake the same morning asking him if he could come and see them on a matter of the utmost urgency.

On sending in his name, he was not kept waiting. The junior partner received him in his private room, and then took him along to the senior partner, Wallingford Harborough, one of the best-known and most conservative financial forces in the City.

Both partners were just past middle age, clean-shaven, remarkably similar in height, which was medium, crispness of manner, and mode of dress, each affecting a plain ensemble of dark grey. They were the type of men with whom Blake always found it a pleasure to do business.

"I have brought you in to my partner so that we can make one discussion serve," said Whittaker, when Blake had settled down with a cigar. "What we wish to consult you about is, strictly speaking, in my department; but Harborough knows all about it and, indeed, it was his suggestion that we consult you."

"Nothing very serious, I hope?" remarked Blake.

"We are not in position to pass an opinion yet; but, if it is as we fear, then it is most serious —most serious, Mr. Blake. I shall be as brief as possible. It concerns primarily certain post-War debentures of one of the small monarchies that has emerged from the general shake-up in Eastern Europe —Polonia, to be exact."

"Yes —I know it quite well, although I have only been there once since it was created an independent state."

"I take it that you are in touch with conditions there, then, and will know of the twenty million pound loan which Polonia floated last year?"

"Of course. Let me see. I believe that the loan was in the form of an issue of debentures following on the funding of the debt to this country and America?"

"Quite right. It was divided among the principal allies, but England and America sponsored most of it. France was responsible for two millions; Italy for two millions, and Belgium for one million. That left fifteen millions, of which this country sponsored eight millions, and America seven millions. The issue was in the form of six percent. bearer bonds, guaranteed jointly by the above-named countries. From an issue point of view it was a great success, for Polonia is being run on sound lines, and her credit is good. The issue was over-subscribed some five or six times.

"Now then. I may say that this firm handled a good many of those bonds at the time. In fact, I think I should be safe in saying that we were the principal dealers both at the time of the issue and after, for they immediately went to a premium. More than that, dealing has been very active in those bonds ever since the issue. For what is, after all, a small, obscure country, the bonds have commanded a most surprisingly wide market.

"We have had our share of the business, but dealings have not been confined to any one particular firm. Until last night, I could not have told you the total of these dealings over the past three months, but this morning I can do so, for our accountants have prepared a statement, and it is most surprisingly large considering that only eight millions were floated on this market.

"You may wonder what inspired me to have that list prepared. I will tell you. It is the same thing that caused us to telephone to you. It begins with the day before yesterday. During the morning of that day we had a visitor, a Mr. Cornelius Van Tromp, of New York. This gentleman is a client of our New York correspondents, and brought from them a letter of introduction to us, as well as a letter of credit for a large amount drawn by them on us.

"We naturally received him with every attention, and he lunched with me the same day. After lunch we came on here, for he wished to receive some money against his letter of credit, and it was when that business was completed he asked me to sell some Polonia bonds on his account. Our New York people had handled a good many of them on that side, just as we had here.

"I told him, of course, that we should be pleased to do so, and he then handed me a bundle of the debentures to the total of five thousand pounds. Just as exchange between London and New York was at the time, there was a slight advantage to him to sell in London, which I mention in passing, just to show that Mr. Cornelius Van Tromp knew what he was about."

"One moment, please," broke in Blake. "What were the face values of the bonds; or were they all the same?"

"All the same —one hundred pounds each. The whole Polonian issue was the same."

"Thank you. Proceed, please."

"Nothing was easier than to sell, for, as I have remarked, the bonds command a good and free market. I made a personal matter of it, and later that afternoon, just before the Stock Exchange closed, I happened to meet another member, who is a personal friend of mine. I asked him casually if he wanted some Polonians, and it just happened that he chanced to be in the market. He mentioned three thousand, but when I told him I had one lot of five thousand to sell he said he would take them.

"Early yesterday morning, that is as regards business in the City, I sent a bundle of bonds across to Hilton and Morris —Morris being the partner to whom I had spoken. Our clerk brought back an acknowledgment slip from them and the transfer was at once credited in the account which we had opened in Mr. Van Tromp's name.

"So far everything was all right. But just before twelve o'clock, Dave Morris came personally to see me. He brought with him not only the bundle of bonds which I had sent him, but another parcel as well. This other parcel consisted of two thousand pounds in Polonian debentures which they were holding on behalf of a client, and among them were several series numbers exactly similar to others in the packet handed to me by Mr. Cornelius Van Tromp!"

"Ah! Unless the bonds had been duplicated through some carelessness in printing, then one suspects just one thing," remarked Blake.

"Exactly. Forgery!"

"Do you suspect that in this case?"

"I do, and I shall explain why. Naturally I could not understand it at all; nor could Morris. We came into my partner and the three of us tried to hammer out some explanation. We took into account, naturally, what you mentioned just now —the possibility of duplication through carelessness. But we soon settled that doubt by sending for the secretary of the Polonian ministry, who had the full records of the issue. He was able to prove beyond doubt that the series numbers could not have been duplicated, for the issue was checked and cross-checked in Polonia, and certified by their own Government Bank. He naturally wanted to know what was up, for he smelled a rat. We put him off for the time being, and then got busy with the cable to our New York correspondents.

"We could not but have suspicions against Van Tromp, but there seemed no room for such when we got our answer from New York. Mr. Van Tromp has been a client of theirs for many years; is a very wealthy man whose character is beyond suspicion. His holding of Polonian bonds was bought through our New York correspondents, and he made no change in that holding until he took about half his holding away when he sailed for Europe. And yet the fact remained that some of the series numbers of the bonds he had given us to sell were exactly similar to those held by Hilton and Morris.

"What to do next? Had the issue not been of bearer bonds, our procedure would have been comparatively simple. When the bonds were presented for the transfer to be noted, the duplication of the numbers would have been noticed at once. But not so in his case.

"In the meantime, I sent a note to Mr. Van Tromp asking him to call and see me, and yesterday afternoon I got out all the Polonian bonds we ourselves were holding on behalf of different clients, just to check up the series numbers. It was then I got another shock, for among them I found no fewer than seven with series number exactly similar to others in the packet which Van Tromp had handed me. Seven is not a large number, but take it in conjunction with only fifty bonds brought here from New York, and considering that Hilton and Morris also had duplicate numbers, the duplication appears most serious.

"In other words, the chances of there being seven duplicate numbers among those we held, and other duplicate numbers among those held by Hilton and Morris —only two of the firms that have dealt in them —then, one cannot help but suspect that there may be a very large number of duplicates about; and if one eliminates the idea of this duplication being the result of carelessness in printing, then one comes back to the one thing before mentioned —"

"Forgery," supplied Blake.

"Exactly!"

"Does Mr. van Tromp know all this?"

"Not all; but we had to take him into our confidence to a certain extent. I am satisfied that he is all right."

"In that case, then, it would seem that if his bonds are genuine, the duplicate numbers which you hold and which are held by Hilton and Morris must be forgeries."

"That is the suspicion."

"Have you made comparisons?"

"Naturally. But we cannot distinguish between them. Either might be genuine, either might be a forgery."

"But surely that could be determined by an expert examination?"

"We believe so. That is exactly why we decided to consult you before going any further. If they are forgeries —if such bonds have been afloat for some time past —then one can only assume that the forgery has been carried out on a very big scale."

"One question just here. The bonds which you received from Mr. van Tromp were all, I understand, part and parcel of the quota of issue which was allotted to the New York market originally?"

"Yes. Both he and our New York people have confirmed that."

"In that case, these bonds can only be part of the official consignment sent through by the fiscal agents who acted on behalf of the Government of Polonia?"

"Exactly!"

"Who did act in that capacity?"

"In the first instance it was the State Bank in Polonia. In London the English allotment was handled by Keever & Co. I understand they also — What is it, Mr. Blake?"

Whittaker had broken off to make this remark as Blake suddenly sat bolt upright.

"Nothing —nothing at all. I beg your pardon for interrupting you. Proceed, please."

Both Whittaker and Harborough were still looking at the detective a little queerly, but at Blake's assurance and apology the junior partner continued:

"Keever & Co. handled the French allocation, too, I believe. I take it they would also look after the Belgian quota, but I cannot say who handled the bonds in Italy. In New York the distributing house was Morrison, Greening & Co.; and our own correspondents, Baker & Starr, disposed of a large proportion of the American quota."

"I see. That is something I shall make a note of. Now, another query. When you found certain series numbers had been duplicated, did you extend your investigation in order to discover if this duplication pertained to bonds issued here in England?"

"That possibility, naturally, was in my mind; but so far I have not discovered anything of the sort."

"In other words, then, the duplication, as far as you know at present, exists only in connection with certain bonds sold here in England, and others which were originally issued in America?"

"Yes."

"So, assuming that Mr. van Tromp had not walked into your office with a parcel of these bonds, which he wished you to sell in this market, the existence of duplicate series numbers might not have been discovered for some time; or, say, until other bonds from America may have drifted into the London market which might have presented the same peculiar features."

The senior partner spoke for the first time.

"I follow Mr. Blake's point. It is sound. He means that as things stand now it looks as if certain Polonian bonds had been put out on our market here which bear duplicate series numbers to bonds which were floated in New York as part of the original issue; that, if we assume the American bonds to be genuine then, eliminating the possibility of duplication through carelessness in printing, all the duplicate numbers on the London market must be the forgeries —not those issued in New York."

"You have my point perfectly," said Blake. "And if we do accept the possibility of forgery, then it means that the London market was selected to receive the forgeries, and that series numbers of bonds issued in New York were chosen deliberately as least likely to lead to discovery. This point is a most important one, and, taken in conjunction with the fact that up to now you cannot indicate any certain flaw to distinguish the forged bonds from the genuine, I think we can take it that we are up against something very big."

"You have all the facts we can supply," remarked Whittaker. "What do you suggest, Mr. Blake?"

"I shall want to give some thought to the matter."

"But you will take up the case, will you not?"

"I see no reason why I should not do so. What about Scotland Yard?"

"We have said nothing yet, nor shall we do so at present if you are working on it. To our mind it is a case for private investigation before the Public Prosecutor is notified. You see, we haven't proved yet that the duplicate bonds are forgeries. Moreover, no one is under suspicion. We have just touched the outside edge of the mystery, as it were, and as soon as we began to feel sure that something was wrong we decided to call you in."

"What about Hilton and Morris?"

"They are naturally very anxious, but will do nothing without consulting us. They knew we are taking you into our confidence, and are at your disposal if you have anything to ask them. If those bonds are forgeries, and there has been any large amount floated —why, don't you see the complications that are going to arise, Mr. Blake? It is a most serious thing, and may have very far-reaching effects."

"I see that plainly enough. If the forgeries run to any great quantity, I should think it would affect every firm that had dealings in them; and if such a thing gets whispered abroad every holder of those bonds will demand an accounting and a checking up."

"Which would mean a panic in Polonian securities," put in the senior partner. "The market would be flooded with the bonds of that country, and with a suspicion of forgery about no one would risk buying them. The Secretary to the Ministry realises this, and for that reason will keep quiet until we know where we stand."

"Very well, gentlemen. I will take the case. And you can depend that I shall lose no time in getting to work. But there are a few points on which I shall require information —to-day if possible. I shall write them down and give them to you."

"I can promise you that every scrap of information we can get together is at your service," responded Whittaker.

Blake nodded, and, taking out his fountain-pen, drew a blank pad of paper towards him. He wrote for some minutes, while the two partners watched him closely, each thinking as they did so that there was a feeling of confidence to be gained from just looking at the strong sweep of that clean-cut jaw.

When Blake had finished he pushed the pad back.

"Just those," he remarked. "And one thing more. Can I take with me two of the bonds bearing the same series numbers —that is, one which must be genuine and one which we believe must be a forgery?"

"Certainly! Anything else?"

"Well, it might be as well if you gave me a note of introduction to Mr. van Tromp. I don't know that I want to look him up, but I might."

"I shall write one in my room if you will come with me," said Whittaker.

And so, provided with what he had requested, Sexton Blake took his departure some ten minutes later, with a strong inward feeling that this new case of the forged bonds was going to be one of the biggest issues he had embarked upon for some time past.

Moreover, he was right.

THE FIFTH CHAPTER.

The Two Straws.

TWO days later Sexton Blake and his assistant, Tinker, were in the laboratory where Blake was just completing certain exhaustive analyses and chemical tests on which he had been engrossed for the past thirty-six hours.

On the enamelled, glass-topped experimenting table at which he sat was an array of spirit-lamps, test-tubes, white enamelled dishes of various sizes and depths, glass rods, steel rods, measuring phials, bottles of liquids of almost every conceivable colour, two microscopes —one being very powerful, with a magnifying power of more than three thousand —a black box fitted with a complicated system of wires and coils.

At his elbow were several engraved and printed certificates, which a close examination would have shown to be bearer bonds of the state of Polonia, each of a nominal face value of one hundred pounds. And in the widest of the enamelled dishes, two more of the bonds were at soak; but in their case most of the green printing and gilt decoration had disappeared through the action of various acids with which Blake had treated them.

But it was a small square cut from those two that was holding the keen attention of Blake and Tinker, the latter listening closely while his master discoursed.

"With just the two bonds which Mr. Whittaker handed me the other morning I could not be sure, my lad. It needed these additional tests. But now, with the results we have before us, I can pass a definite opinion."

"You mean that the duplicate bonds are forgeries as you suspected, guv'nor?"

"Exactly. And it is a long time, my lad, since I have come across anything quite so interesting from a professional point of view. I have investigated a good many cases of forgery in the past; you have assisted me in the analyses of a considerable variety of both genuine and forged banknotes. But this case is quite unique. A care has been exercised in the selection of every single item, which is amazing, indicating a wonderful brain capacity for detail behind the whole thing.

"I do not speak only of the exact methods of engraving and printing. They are of the highest order, and I am not sure that I should be prepared to pronounce certain of the documents forgeries on just that. The choice of paper, too, has been remarkable in the care used. Until this afternoon I was almost certain that the paper was off the same piles from which that for the genuine bonds was taken. It looked as if someone in the engravers or Treasury department in Polonia had been an accomplice.

"I am not so sure that there hasn't been betrayal on the inside in the supply of inks and designs; the work is so utterly perfect. But as to the paper I can now state with absolute confidence that it is not the same, although the difference is only perceptible in the very smallest degree measurable by certain very delicate and difficult chemical tests. It is a question of reaction speed which is practically infinitesimal, but which does exist."

"I can't see any difference in the paper, guv'nor. I have followed your analyses closely, and even in the big microscope the texture seems absolutely the same; colour appeared identical, and so did thickness and tensile strength. As for the watermark, it is exactly the same in every case, and I can assure you I measured it with the finest instruments we possess."

"Quite so, my lad. There is a difference, nevertheless, although I am willing to concede that ninety-nine analytical chemists out of every hundred would pronounce the samples identical in every respect, and certainly from the same presses or rolls and made from the same lot of pulp. I do not take undue credit to myself in saying that. I made the statement because very few commercial chemists have need to employ the complicated tests which I have applied to these samples."

"Just what is the difference, then, guv'nor?"

"I will tell you. It will explain nothing for you to make a further test of these two squares which I hold. You would find them identical —apparently. And yet I can tell you that, while they were undoubtedly made by exactly the same process, probably in the same mill, and unquestionably one of them used a standard of production, still they differ in one thing. This sample here in my left hand has been made from wheat-straw; the one in my right from oat-straw.

"Ask any ordinary chemist what the difference is between wheat-straw and oat-straw, and he will tell you that there is none, or practically none. He would be almost correct in his statement. The straw of the two grains is of the same fibre and composition. An analysis of two samples as taken from the field during growth would reveal certain slight differences; another series of analyses made after harvest when the straw had dried would also reveal minute degrees of unlikeness, and so on. That is obvious and elementary.

"Therefore, one would think that while these small points might be perceptible when tests were made while the straw was in its natural state, they would disappear or be absorbed during the process of chemical manufacture of paper when the straw was in great bulk, and, in many cases, mixed.

"So it would to the almost indistinguishable point. But there is sufficient knowledge to-day to enable us to detect that infinitesimal difference, and that is what I have succeeded in doing from the tests I have been making.

"This sodden bit of paper in my left hand, the one made from wheat-straw, is that on which the genuine Polonia bonds were produced; this other fragment, that made from oat-straw, is that used for the forgeries. And slight though the difference is, my lad, we have now an infallible test by which we can pronounce beyond the faintest shadow of doubt which of the bonds are genuine and which are not."

"My aunt, guv'nor, as you say, the people behind the forgery must have spent no end of care over the fraud!"

"Care and time, young 'un. It is, as I have said, quite unique in its way. And, so far, just one small thing has come up which seems to give us even a slight clue."

"You mean, guv'nor?"

"The fact that Keever & Co. was the London firm which acted as fiscal agents for the Polonian Government."

"Well, we know what Augustus Keever is; and we know that he is hitched up with Prince von Wadstein, the so-called 'mysterious monseigneur.' And you called Wadstein the biggest and brainiest crook of this generation. Do you think he is behind it? It seems the sort of thing that he might conceive."

"Not so fast, Tinker! It is quite true that we know Augustus Keever to be a crook, and, in that affair at Venice, we established a definite connection with Prince von Wadstein —not to mention the fact we now know the German scientist is the 'mysterious monseigneur.'"

"But that does not bring us to the end of the road. Unless I am greatly mistaken, we have some distance to travel yet. For instance, we must not forget that, with the exception of ourselves and Scotland Yard in this country, Augustus Keever occupies a very strong position, both in the financial and social worlds.

"I grant you that the fact of undoubted forgery which we have established and the coincidence —we may call it that for the moment —that Keever & Co. acted as fiscal agents in England for the Polonian Government in connection with the flotation of the bonds in question, makes it look bad for Keever.

"But beyond the actual fact of forgery, we have proved nothing yet; and we may be sure that, if Keever is guilty, he has covered his tracks with every care. Before we can come into the open and make a direct accusation, we must be able to establish absolute proof of guilt. And that is what I intend to do if such proof can be found.

"The next step is to make a careful analysis of the statement of recent dealings in Polonian bonds which we received this morning from Harborough & Whittaker.

"From a cursory glance it seems to me that transactions have been on a heavy scale when one considers the narrow range of fluctuations in such securities, and remembers that, after all, some eight million pounds in bonds is not a very large amount for this country to absorb. That analysis may open up a fresh channel for exploration. But isn't that the telephone, young 'un? Go along and answer it."

Tinker jumped up and left the laboratory.

He returned in a few minutes, however, and, as Blake glanced up inquiringly from the microscope, the lad said:

"It was Mademoiselle Yvonne. She asked if she could come round now; she wants to see you about something very important."

"And you said?"

"I told her you would be delighted to see her," responded the lad with a grin. "So she is on her way now."

To which Blake made no rejoinder.

Suddenly Blake turned and regarded her. . . . Yvonne guessed what was going on in Blake's mind, and she put out her hand and touched his.

THE SIXTH CHAPTER.

Two Visitors and Two Letters.

BLAKE and Tinker had scarcely finished washing away the stains of "stinks", when Yvonne arrived, bringing Nirvana in tow — an intention which she had communicated to the lad over the phone, but which he had not thought it necessary to pass on to Blake. He knew, however, that Blake would have something to say about it later.

When the two girls were seated Blake looked at Yvonne quizzically.

"What is this matter of importance you wish to see me about?"

Yvonne had lighted one of the Russian cigarettes which Blake always kept by him, but which he rarely smoked and, curiously enough, were the same brand favoured by Yvonne. She smiled at him through a thin waft of smoke.

"I am afraid I —we need your advice," she responded. "I think it will be better if I tell you exactly what occurred two days ago and why, on the same evening, I took the law into my own hands."

Blake frowned.

"I thought you had given up that sort of thing," he said shortly. "You know what difficulties there were the last time?"

"But this was entirely different," she protested, woman-like. "Wait until I tell you the whole thing."

Forthwith, she began and related what had occurred between her and Augustus Keever at the Venetia. She then explained how she had come to the conclusion that the best thing to do would be to strike at Keever before he could put his machinery into motion. That entailed a full description of the burglary she and Nirvana had committed at Keever's house and, of course, a confession of their discovery and certain recognition by Keever, Marie and Philippe the Fox.

Blake listened in silence to the story. When she had finished he eyed her sternly.

"The whole thing was a mistake," he said, after he had treated Nirvana to a disapproving glance as well. "Whatever you may think Keever is —no matter who you may know he is —you were playing a dangerous game when you went to his house as you did. Scotland Yard may have its doubts about Augustus Keever and feel convinced that the man is following criminal ways; but, even so, that is not going to incline them to encourage burglary on your part. And, moreover, the actual attack upon the negro butler combined with the use of a drug, and then the binding and gagging of the fellow, adds materially to the seriousness of the whole affair. You know that quite as well as I."

"I agree with every word you say." drawled Yvonne, her eyes not at all as serious as they should have been. "And, what is more, Mr. Keever makes the same point. I have received a letter from him which is an odd mixture of plain roguery and pious threats. He lays great stress on the same points which you have raised."

"Keever is no fool," muttered Blake. "I take it that it is this letter which has induced you to come and see me."

"Partly that and partly something else. I have yet to tell you one thing. I have already said that I found in Keever's safe a paper which is of considerable importance to Nirvana. If what is in that document is true, then Augustus Keever did not lie to me at the Venetia when he said that this time he really did possess definite information of the whereabouts of Nirvana's father.

"But I have not yet confessed that in the confusion of the moment, when Keever and the others were coming along the hall, I took other things as well from the safe. I did not know what they were at the time, but on reaching home I discovered they were certain bonds which Keever had been discussing with Marie and Philippe the Fox. I was puzzled then, and I am still puzzled about them; nor does Keever's letter enlighten me."

At the mention of bonds in connection with Keever's name, Blake and Tinker looked at each other, but Blake said nothing yet.

"I determined to force Keever to make the next move. He did so when he wrote, but I think you will agree when you have read his letter that he is in a considerable stew. He blusters a lot, but he can't conceal what he is really feeling. I don't know why he should reveal such perturbation, but in view of it all I should like your advice before taking any action —if you will give it to me."

"Have you brought the letter with you?"

"Yes —his last letter, the document relating to Nirvana which I took from the safe and one of the bonds."

Yvonne began to open her bag as she spoke, and while she was still fumbling within. Blake said:

"I should like to ask one question about those bonds before you bring them out?"

Yvonne paused and glanced up. "Yes?"

"Are they, by any chance, bearer bonds of the Polonian Government?"

"Why —yes. How did you guess?"

"I'll explain later. Let me have a look at the letter and the document relating to Nirvana. We shall examine the bonds after."

Yvonne was considerably intrigued at Blake's words but, knowing him as she did, she did not press for an explanation but drew out first the blue envelope containing the document relating to Nirvana. She handed it to Blake, who spread it out on his desk and bent his head over it.

Silence reigned in the consulting-room for the better part of ten minutes while Blake read and re-read what purported to be a letter from someone in France, presumably a private agent of Keever's, giving him a report on the finding of a person whom Keever had instructed him to find. A rough translation of the document made it read as follows:

"Sir, —I have now to report success in the mission with which you charged me. The clue which I secured from various data supplied by you has led me to a person who, I am certain, is he whom you seek.

"I have ascertained that he lived in London some twenty years ago and was married there to a lady who, at the time, was one of the principal dancers in the Russian ballet which was creating a furore in England.

"There were four children of the marriage one of whom died in infancy. The remaining three consisted of a boy and two girls. The person whom I have discovered was then and is now an engraver and dry-point artist by profession. I have not yet gained his confidence sufficiently to learn why he left his family and has not communicated with them since that time. That will take a little time longer; but I can assure you that it is the man you seek.

"I shall proceed with further investigations and should you desire to interview him I can make the necessary arrangements.

"I enclose formal particulars together with an account of expenses up to date, and should be obliged for a further remittance at your convenience,

"I am, sir, etc.,
"HENRI PASCAL."

"Quite an interesting document —if it is genuine," was Blake's comment as he looked up.

"If it is genuine! Do you doubt its authenticity?"

"Well, it would be unwise to place too much dependence on any claim which Augustus Keever might make. He is quite capable of devising a paper of this sort against the chance of an occasion cropping up when he could use it to advantage. But, for the moment, we shall regard it as quite genuine. It refers to someone whom Keever has been seeking; that much is obvious. How do you know this person referred to is Nirvana's father?"

"Keever says so in the letter which came to-day."

"Ah! Am I to read that as well?"

"Of course. That is why we came to see you. Here it is!"

Yvonne passed over another envelope and, taking out the folded sheet of thick double paper it contained. Blake again began to read. There was no ambiguity about this communication.

"Dear Miss Cartier." it ran, "I am willing to confess that I cannot understand why I have heard nothing from you since the surprise visit you paid my house two nights ago. If your purpose in coming was to gain possession of a certain letter, then I freely acknowledge that your effort was wholly successful.

"In a way it was fair enough, for war had been declared between us —a challenge which I accepted. I have no complaint to make against any methods you might have employed in order to secure that letter; but I do protest against the deliberate rifling of my safe.

"Just recollect, dear lady, that you have committed a double felony in the eyes of the law of this country; and, despite what Scotland Yard may feel for the victim, they do not condone that sort of thing. Felony is not a nice term; nor is burglary! nor robbery under arms; nor armed assault. And yet all these apply to you.

"I refer, of course, to certain bonds which you also abstracted from my safe. I find, on checking over the list which was attached to the bundle, that you have taken no less than nine of those bonds to the value of nine hundred pounds. If you found yourself in monetary difficulties, and wherein need of a loan, I should have been most happy to accommodate you to the extent of a much larger sum than those bonds represent. And I am still prepared to do so.

"But, in any event, those bonds must be returned to me within twenty-four hours of the receipt of this letter, for the reason that I hold them in trust for another person, and must therefore be prepared to make an accounting, should I be called upon to do so.

"I think you will see the fairness and reason of this, and meet my request. If not, I warn you that I shall not hesitate to go to the police and lay a charge against you. It rests entirely with you whether I do so or not.

"As regards the letter which you took and which, you have no doubt guessed by now, refers to Nirvana, that is a different matter. In this I have a definite proposal to make, which, if you have Nirvana's interests at heart, as you profess to have, you will certainly agree to. It is this:

"I told you at the Venetia that I had in truth located Nirvana's father. The letter which you have abstracted from my safe is proof of my statement. I promised Nirvana that I would take her to her father, and this time I mean it. I pass my word of honour that I shall keep my promise.

"I am going to France in a day or two, and if this offer is accepted Nirvana may accompany me. I am also willing to give an undertaking that in no way will she be importuned by her sister or anyone else; that she will not be asked to undertake anything that may be distasteful to her; and, furthermore, in order to prove my bona fides, I am willing that you should accompany her, if you desire to do so. This is a firm offer, to which I must have a reply, as in the other matter, within twenty-four hours.

"If my plans are put forward, I shall probably telephone you during the course of the day on which you should receive this. Should you choose to ignore my two conditions entirely, I assure you that I shall certainly go to Scotland Yard and charge you on two different counts.

"If it is to continue to be war, I am quite prepared. If it is to be a temporary armistice —if you wish to term it that —I shall be equally amenable. One thing or the other it must be.

"I am, dear Miss Cartier,

"Yours most faithfully, "AUGUSTUS KEEVER."

Blake passed the letter across to Tinker to read; then he sat frowning at his desk. He was debating just how much or how little he should tell Yvonne about his latest case.

Had Yvonne been alone he would not have hesitated to take her into his entire confidence. But Nirvana was present, and, while no one felt more kindly towards her than Blake, he could not forget that only recently she had been the associate of Marie and Keever — unwillingly, it is true; but, nevertheless, if she fell into their power again there would be ways of making her talk.

He did not mistrust her. She had proved her loyalty to Tinker again and again at no small peril to herself, and on the last occasion, in Venice,[2] it had come near to costing her her life. Still, there was the shadow of Keever and Marie and Philippe the Fox hanging over her. While Yvonne controlled her movements things were safe enough. It was the other contingency he had to consider.

Suddenly he turned his head and regarded her under level brows.

There was no denying that she looked very dainty and very beautiful as she sat there, with a shaft of late afternoon sunlight streaming against her golden hair. Her eyes were a little puzzled as she looked back at Blake.

Inwardly, Nirvana was a little afraid of Sexton Blake. And instinct told her now that it was she who was a problem of some sort to him. A sharp feeling of intense longing surged over her to try and make this man of steel believe that she would rather die than bring one tiny grain of wrong to him or to Tinker.

She had always felt that he tolerated her only for Tinker's sake — that he would have been better pleased had she never entered Tinker's life. It was just that feeling that, time and again, had caused her to leave Tinker without news of her —to fight her dreary fight alone, rather than to have the lad run any risk on her behalf.

For once in his life Sexton Blake had not probed the real depths of character of a human being with whom he was in contact, and it was just because Blake was human enough to have been predisposed against Nirvana because of the criminal circle into which she had been swept.

It is just possible that he may also have been human enough to feel a slight twinge of jealousy towards the person who had undoubtedly drawn forth from Tinker a regard such as the lad had never felt before. It was entirely different from the loyal love he felt

---

[2] The Mystery of the Venetian Palace, 1201. . . /drf

for Blake, and he had proved the worth of that by following his loyalty to Blake instead of the desire of his heart, when the two had been weighed in the balance.

Yvonne guessed what was going on in Blake's mind, for suddenly she put out her hand and touched his.

No one living knew the inmost workings of the man, Sexton Blake, as did Yvonne. He drew his gaze from Nirvana and found Yvonne smiling at him. She did not speak; she had no need. To Blake it was perfectly plain that she was saying:

"Don't mistrust her any longer; she will never betray you. I know she is solid gold all through, and you know I should never jeopardise your interests."

Blake smiled back at her, and then he flashed a kindly look at Nirvana.

Even Tinker had sensed what was going on in his mind, for he suddenly realised the lad was gazing at him questioningly.

In that moment Blake made his decision, and —

Tr-r-r-ring!

The telephone-bell shrilled impatiently, and the decision remained unspoken.

THE SEVENTH CHAPTER.

The Chase is On.

"IS that Mr. Sexton Blake?" asked the voice at the other end of the wire.

"Yes. Who are you, please?"

"This is Stanley Whittaker speaking, Mr. Blake. Did you get those figures I sent on to you this morning?"

"About the transaction during the past few days? Yes; but I have not had time to go into them yet. I was just about to begin when someone came."

"Well, I can amplify those figures now. Have you seen an evening paper?"

"Not yet."

"When you do you will see that Polonias are down no less than seven points on the day. In the case of the bonds of any Government that, as you well know, is a disastrous fall."

"It certainly is. Can you tell me the cause?"

"It looks to me as if there had been a leakage some place. I know that the bonds have been freely offered during the day, and have done my best to discover from what source they were coming. So far, I have been unable to do so. But I have secured one thing that may prove of considerable importance."

"What is it?"

"During the afternoon session we were offered Polonias by a certain small outside firm. It came to me personally, and I said that we could probably take the parcel. I asked for them to be sent across to us, and said that I should either complete or return them tomorrow morning. I wanted to get them into my hands in order to compare the serial numbers with those we held and the list of series numbers of those in the possession of Hilton & Morris.

"Well, Mr. Blake, among the lot I came across two that were exactly the same series numbers as two of those which Mr. Cornelius Van Tromp had offered us. Doesn't that look as if they might be forgeries?"

"It certainly does," responded Blake quickly. "That is a most important discovery. Have you the packet by you?"

"Yes."

"I wonder if you would entrust it to me for to-night? I can promise to send it on to you in the morning to reach your office before the Exchange opens."

"I was going to suggest the same thing. I have a man standing by, and they will be in your hands under the hour."

"Excellent! And now I have some important information for you. I have to-day completed my analyses of those which you handed me, and I have discovered a distinct difference in the paper. It is very, very small, but it is sufficient to prove what you suggested."

"You mean forgery."

"I do."

"You have done more than I dared hope for, Mr. Blake. Have you any clue as to the person or persons concerned?"

"I have a strong suspicion, which I hope to strengthen before this night is out. I cannot say more now, but you can take it from me that things will march quickly within the next few hours. I may find it necessary to leave London suddenly, and if I do I shall get in touch with you before I go."

"Please do, if possible. I shall get those bonds started at once."

Blake re-hung the receiver and turned to Yvonne.

"You mentioned some bonds," he said. "I suggested that they might be bonds issued by the Polonian Government. May I look at them now?"

"Yes; but should I not tell you first what I overheard Augustus Keever saying to Marie and Philippe the Fox about bonds?"

"By all means! The conversation I have just heard over the phone was apropos of something which I shall tell you presently. Now, what did Keever say?"

Briefly, Yvonne related what she and Nirvana had overheard when they stood concealed behind the curtain in Keever's study. Blake nodded in a satisfied way when she had finished.

"The person to whom I have just been speaking has given me one important bit of information. What you tell me strengthens the avenue which that opened up. You may well look puzzled, Yvonne. Let me see those bonds, please. You will understand matters better before you go."

Yvonne took the bonds from her bag, and the moment she lay them on the desk Blake saw that they were exactly similar in appearance to the bonds which had engrossed his attention during the past thirty-six hours. He gave the actual engraving only a cursory inspection. What he examined closely were the series numbers, jotting them down on a pad of blank paper as he came to them.

When he had noted all nine he pushed them aside and opened a drawer. From this he took a list of series numbers with which Whittaker had supplied him, and these he compared with those he had just written down. He found no duplicates, however, and was a little disappointed, although he realised that the chances of doing so, considering the large number issued, were very small.

And now he told Yvonne fully just what it all meant, knowing as he did that he was allowing Nirvana to learn that which Keever would give a great deal to learn. It took some time for him to finish the relation, and, indeed, he was just on the last lap, so to say, when the front-door bell rang.

Tinker rose to answer it, and returned in a few moments bearing a sealed packet. After one glance, in which he noted the name of Harborough & Whittaker on the envelope, Blake knew that it must be the packet of bonds which Whittaker had said he was sending on. He held it in his hand until he had finished the story of the case, then, as he broke the seal, he remarked:

"We shall just have a look at these. I want to compare them with the nine you brought."

His three listeners bent forward in intense silence as Blake laid the bonds out and began to compare the series number with those which Yvonne had abstracted from Keever's safe. And before he had come to the third one his fist hit the desk softly as he exclaimed:

"We've got him! Got him, without the shadow of a doubt!"

"Do you really mean —" began Yvonne.

"I mean that these bonds which were offered in the City to-day are unquestionably part of those which were in Keever's safe when you opened it. The series numbers are not duplicates, but they are of the same group as those on the bonds which you brought.

"It is absolute proof that these bonds were those which Keever was speaking of to Marie and Philippe the Fox. It is these bonds which those two have been offering on the market during the past two days. And that gives a definite connection between these bonds and those of which I told you. Now that I have found the correct chemical test I can prove further whether these bonds are genuine or forged. If they are forged, then the whole chain is complete, for the fact that Keever & Co. acted as fiscal agents for the Polonian Government will then become a most condemning fact."

"Then does that mean you can make an open arrest of Keever?"

"Not yet —not yet; but I shall. We must move very cautiously. We can't even guess how many of these forged bonds have been disposed of. There is that to be discovered and the complicated question of responsibility to fix.

"It involves every brokerage house and bank that dealt in them. It is one of the worst tangles I have ever encountered. But it must be unravelled. This which we now feel sure of is but a beginning. Keever has not embarked on such a gigantic fraud without planning with the utmost care; and I have a feeling that other brains, as well, are behind it."

"You mean Von Wadstein?"

"Yes. And furthermore, Whittaker has just advised me that there has been a heavy slump in Polonias to-day. In what are supposed to be gilt-edged government bonds of trustee class that is a very bad sign. It means that suspicion is leaking out somewhere —the last thing I wanted to happen until I was ready to act. What effect that will have on Keever's movements I can't tell. He says in his letter to you that he is planning to go abroad soon. This may precipitate his movements. If so, there is no time to lose."

Blake was pacing up and down, forgetful, for the moment, that he was not talking only to Tinker. It was Yvonne's voice that recalled him.

"Let us discuss that letter, please! I have a suggestion to make."

"What is it?"

"You said the letter referring to Nirvana's father —I mean the one which presumably came to Keever from Paris —might be only a faked letter got up by Keever. On the other hand, it may be genuine. But which ever is the case, it shows that he intended making a strong effort to get Nirvana to go back to them, and in this letter which he wrote to me that is really the chief burden of what he has to say. If things are coming to a crisis with him, as you suggest, it may be possible then that he must have been planning for some time past to make his getaway. Don't you agree?"

"Most assuredly. A man with Keever's financial interests could not clear out at a few hours' notice. And when Keever does go it means that he goes for good. He would never be able to return to this country."

"I know that. And that is why I think he must set very great store on getting Nirvana back in order to be able to devote so much time to the subject when other worries must be driving him."

"You argue soundly, Yvonne. And that means you have a suggestion at the back of your mind. What is it?"

"It is that you let me come in on this case with you. It is that you agree to my letting Augustus Keever know that I accept his proposals, and that both Nirvana and I will join him when he leaves England. In this way you will have a direct connection with him, no matter where he may be."

"But what about the danger to you?"

"You may trust me to look after myself," she returned confidently.

"And Nirvana, too," Yvonne assured him. "I have been thinking of this ever since you told me about the bonds. I think it would be a strong move, and I want you to say 'Yes.' "

Blake was reluctant, but Yvonne was persistent.

At the end of half an hour she had got him to say that he would think it over that night and give her his decision in the morning. So at this it was left, and soon after Yvonne and Nirvana took their departure.

AT half-past nine that evening a letter arrived by special messenger for Blake, and when he tore it open he found a second missive enclosed, for Tinker. His own, he saw at once, was from Yvonne. When he had read it he frowned in sharp annoyance, for it said:

"Shortly after we reached the flat A. K. telephoned, saying that unexpected events made it necessary for him to leave for the Continent to-night.

"He asked for an immediate decision, and I said that I had decided to accept his offer —that Nirvana would go on the condition that I should accompany her.

"He agreed to this, and is picking us up here at the flat at nine o'clock. I am deliberately holding this back so that you cannot receive it before we leave, because I have a feeling that you would try to prevent it.

48

"I have no idea how or by what route we shall travel, but be sure that I shall communicate with you in some way you will understand and as often as is possible. Please watch the 'Agony' columns of London and Paris papers, on the chance that it may be through that medium, although I hope it will be direct. Don't be angry with me. I promise you I shall be careful. And tell Tinker not to worry, for I shall not let Nirvana out of my sight for a single moment. Y."

There was plenty in that note to give Sexton Blake powerfully to think, but nothing stood out with greater force than the fact that Augustus Keever was even then in full flight.

From that moment, for him and Tinker, the chase was on.

The itinerant musician dropped a bit of folded paper in front of the elder peasant as he held out his greasy cap for a few sous.

THE EIGHTH CHAPTER.

Tracked Down!

ONE sunny, crisp morning just eleven days after Sexton Blake had received Yvonne's note informing him that she was deliberately putting her head into the jaws of the tiger, two peasants sat on the terrace of a small cafe in the village of Uxes, in Luxembourg. Almost at their feet was a small muddy stream, the opposite bank of which was German soil.

The two peasants —one a stooped, elderly man, and the other a dark-skinned youth —had reached the village on foot some two days previously. Each had appeared dusty and begrimed with the marks of long journeying afoot, and each carried his few worldly possessions in a shoulder-pack.

Naturally, on their arrival, they were at once the cynosure of all eyes, for strangers who passed more than a night in that little village were rare. But as their first care was to visit the office of the local magistrate in order to have their papers scrutinised and stamped, and since these documents were in perfect order —showing that Franz Coppens and his nephew, Piet Coppens, were respectable Flemish workmen travelling on foot from the Palatinate to their home in Belgium —the suspicion of the villagers of Uxes was allayed.

Moreover, they were popular at the little inn, for, although they spent sparingly, their money was always ready. The elder of the two lads, it seemed, injured a foot just before reaching Uxes, hence the decision to rest for a few days before proceeding.

Had the good soul of the inn dreamed for a single moment that the two peasants were none other than a certain famous London detective and his assistant, she would have had food for gossip for many a long day to come. But she didn't know that, and so careful were the two in every trick of speech and manner, even when alone, that not the faintest suspicion got abroad. Sexton Blake knew how completely all his plans would be shattered if that happened.

Their arrival at Uxes had not been through mere chance.

To explain it, it is necessary to say what led up to it.

AS soon as Blake had learned from Yvonne's note that Augustus Keever was in full flight —had started for the Continent that very night, and that Yvonne and Nirvana were going with him —he had lost no time in getting into action.

He and Tinker had driven at once to Scotland Yard, where they had been fortunate enough to find Sir Henry Fairfax, the Commissioner. That gentleman had sent at once for Detective-Inspector Thomas, and no time had been lost in warning every railway station, every seaport, and every aerodrome to be on the watch for the fugitives.

But swiftly as Blake had acted, Keever must have secured sufficient start to get clear of England before the net was out, for although every possible place was watched and every outward bound passenger scrutinised by keen eyes, not a trace of Keever was the result.

As for Yvonne and Nirvana, they had disappeared as utterly as if they had left the planet.

The following day had been a strenuous one for Blake. The sharp drop in the quotation for Polonia bonds had not been checked, and a small panic struck the market.

All sorts of rumours were flying about, and it was not long before the name of Keever & Co. began to be used in the gossip. By afternoon it was generally known that Augustus Keever was not to be found, that matters with the different companies he controlled were in a very bad state, that Keever was wanted by Scotland Yard, was a fugitive from justice, and so on and so on.

But the thing that sent Polonias rocketting down at a dizzy rate was the official announcement that, through the instrumentality of Mr. Sexton Blake, the well-known criminologist, an injunction had been applied for and granted against all dealings of Keever & Co.

By this time the telephone at Baker Street was ringing frantically and the pavement in front of the house was jammed with an ever-growing crowd, each one of whom was clamouring for a sight of and word from Sexton Blake, the detective and his assistant, Tinker, were already in Paris.

And there they were stalled for eight long days while Blake, assisted by the Paris Surete, put into movement every conceivable bit of machinery he could utilise in trying to track down Keever. He knew that where he found Keever there would he discover traces of

Yvonne and Nirvana; and he knew likewise that in his flight Keever would almost certainly seek the shelter of the powerful "mysterious monseigneur." Therefore it became a concentrated effort to discover the present whereabouts of Prince von Wadstein.

Warned by Yvonne, both Blake and Tinker had kept a careful eye on every possible medium, no matter how bizarre, which might carry a message from her. Not a single thing to encourage them did they see until a week had passed.

And then, from the great heap of papers which were laid in Blake's sitting-room at the Carlitz Hotel, on the Rue de Rivoli, each morning, Tinker came upon a most curious item which had been inserted in a small country "rag" issued in the eastern zone of Luxembourg.

The language, a curious thing in a paper of that sort, was English, and the wording was so ambiguous that it was some little time before Blake discovered what he thought might be a clue. This is how it appeared:

"S. B. refer you to B's D. J. Canto X, stanzas 60, 61, ending second line latter. Hasten. —Y."

The initials "S. B." and "Y." had first caught Tinker's eye, but after several attempts to fathom the meaning of the rest of the message he was forced to give it up. Nor did Blake appear much more successful at first. He pored over it until lunch-time, and during the meal sat in gloomy abstraction, his mind probing, probing, probing into the body of the message.

It would seem, if one took the clue literally, that one was referred to some piece of verse which, Blake reflected, must be of considerable length if it contained ten stanzas and probably more. It then mentioned certain stanzas. In that verse there might be a clue — if the message was from Yvonne. And there was nothing to allay Blake's anxiety in that one final word, "hasten."

After lunch Blake had left the hotel without telling Tinker where he was going, but warning him to remain in their suite. Tinker was idling about, still puzzling over a copy he had made of the two lines, when Blake returned, carrying a small blue volume. Throwing aside his hat and stick, he laid the book on the table and drew up a chair.

"Sit down here, young 'un," he said. "I have a hunch that I have solved the puzzle."

Tinker bent close, eager to see what name was on the volume. His brows went up a little as he read the title —it was Byron's "Don Juan." His gaze then jerked back to the pencilled copy of the message which he had made, and he once more read: "Refer you to B's D. J. Canto X, stanzas 60, 61, ending second line, latter."

"Well, the reference fits all right, my lad," remarked Blake. "The next thing is to find those verses in Canto X, and see if we can make anything of them."

"But what made you think of this book, guv'nor?" asked Tinker, as Blake was turning the pages.

"It had to be some book of verse, and Byron's 'Don Juan' seemed to fit. It may not be this at all that is meant, but we shall soon know. Here we are— Canto X. Let me see. Don Juan starts out on the mission for Catherine of Russia, taking Leila with him. Stanza fifty-nine, sixty —here we are. Listen while I read, and see what you can make of it.

" 'From Poland they came on through Prussia proper,
And Konigsberg, the capital whose vaunt,
Besides some veins of iron, lead, or copper,
Has lately been the great Professor Kant.
Juan, who car'd not a tobacco-stopper
About philosophy, pursued his jaunt
To Germany, whose somewhat tardy millions
Have princes who spur more than their postillions.' "

"So much for stanza 60. Tinker. There are some references in those lines that need thinking over. I believe, young 'un, we are on the right track. But now for the first two lines of stanza 61. Listen."

" 'And thence through Berlin, Dresden, and the like,
Until he reached the castellated Rhine.' "

Blake laid down the book, and rose, repeating more slowly the last line. " 'Until he reached the castellated Rhine.' " Suddenly he paused and thumped the table.

"The meat of the whole thing lies in that last line, Tinker. There is our clue— 'Until he reached the castellated Rhine.' The other stanza was included to convey to us that they had been travelling almost constantly since leaving England, moving from one place to another, which shows they were on the run; but 'castellated Rhine' means that they have come to rest somewhere in that part of Germany, and Yvonne cannot tell us more precisely just where they are."

"Then how on earth are we going to find them, guv'nor? The country drained by the Rhine is enormous. It would take years to cover it."

"Of course. But don't you recall that I said in London I was strongly of the opinion that Keever would seek Von Wadstein?"

"Yes. guv'nor."

"Well, young 'un, it is up to us to discover on what part of the Rhine Prince von Wadstein has an estate, a thing which should be by no means very difficult. As Professor von Wadstein, the prominent German savant, he must have some place as normal headquarters."

"And Yvonne says: 'Hasten!' guv'nor."

"I know, I know, my lad. We shall make a move to-night."

THUS it came about that, some two days later, the two peasants drifted into the village of Uxes. Nor did the innkeeper see any cause for remark in the desire of the elder that they should be given a room on the ground floors his injured foot was sufficient excuse for that.

Nevertheless, that same innkeeper would have been considerably intrigued, somewhere after midnight of the second day's stay of his two peasant guests, had he been able to witness their movements when everyone else in the place was wrapped in slumber.

It was when Blake and Tinker were sitting on the terrace during the morning that an itinerant musician had drifted into the village. As there was a fair on at the time at a neighbouring village, there was nothing remarkable in this, and it was a comparatively simple matter for him to drop a folded bit of paper on the table in front of the elder peasant at the moment he held out his greasy cap for a few sous.

He certainly would never have been taken for one of the ablest sleuths attached to the Paris Surete; but that is exactly what he was, for M. Dupuis, the prefect, had placed five of his best men at Blake's service, and for forty-eight hours they had been combing the Rhine Valley from the borders of Switzerland to the Zuyder Zee in search of an estate where Professor, or Prince von Wadstein might be in residence.

Blake and Tinker retired early to their room.

In doing so they were simply following the example of the whole village. They only removed their outer clothing, and lay down on the covering blankets of the beds. By eleven o'clock the inn was dark and silent, but it was not until the luminous dial of his watch showed the hands at midnight that Blake rose and woke Tinker.

They drew on their clothes silently, and, after thrusting his head through the open window to reconnoitre, Blake led the way over the sill. They found themselves in a small stable yard, paved with rough cobbles. Almost opposite the window through which they had climbed was a gate, which Blake had taken care to inspect during the day.

It was a simple matter to negotiate this, and. once they were over into the lane at the back, there was but a short journey to the outskirts of the village to reach the main highway which was their objective. They were careful to avoid the small bridge, for they knew that Luxembourgoise guards would be on duty at their end, while German guards would be on the other side.

Once clear of the village they travelled at a brisk pace. There was a matter of a couple of miles to cover to the rendezvous, and Blake was anxious to get the business over and return to the inn before there was any chance of their absence being discovered. Any time after three o'clock there was always someone stirring in Uxes, as he had discovered.

The rendezvous was a spot of Blake's own choosing. He had selected it when he had decided to stop at Uxes, and had sent off a message to the nearest of his agents to inform him of it. Therefore it was this spot which was named in the note that had been surreptitiously conveyed to him that morning.

Until one reached that point in the highway the fields on either side were bare, with only a lonely tree here and there looming against the starlit sky. But the spot Blake had selected was a small wood which filled a shallow dip in the land, and when they reached the deep shadow of this Tinker raised his voice in imitation of the hoot of an owl.

The answer came almost immediately after. It appeared to be on the left, and they moved cautiously along in that direction. Suddenly a figure rose up in front of them, and a voice whispered:

"It is you, m'sieu?"

"Yes, Roger. Let us move a little farther into the trees."

"Bien, m'sieu."

They penetrated another ten or twelve yards, and then Blake bent close to the Frenchman.

"What have you found?"

"We have located the place, m'sieu. And it is the spot you seek for. My colleague, Jules, has discovered that a party arrived there some days ago. The members of it correspond to the description furnished by m'sieu."

"English persons? Three women in the party?"

"Oui, m'sieu. Moreover, there is a person whom Jules had no difficulty in recognising as our own French criminal, Philippe the Fox."

"That settles it. What about the person who owns it?"

"The man we shall speak of as the professor? M'sieu, it is his property, and he may be in residence, but, so far, we have been unable to learn for sure. The estate is a large one and well guarded. We are exploring the possibility of bribing some of the servants, but it will be difficult, if possible at all."

"I don't want that done, it is too risky. Where is this place?"

"Not twenty kilometres from where we stand, m'sieu. It is on the bank of the Rhine, very extensive park and forest, and no other dwellings nearer than five kilometres. By morning, m'sieu, I shall have a rough plan of the place, for I am to meet Jules near there at ten o'clock."

"At ten —could you manage to be back here at mid-day?"

"Of a surety, m'sieu!"

"Very well; make another rendezvous here for that hour. You will find us waiting."

"Bien, m'sieu!"

With that, the French detective stole away, and when he had had plenty of chance to reach the highway Blake and Tinker retraced their way to the inn.

Blake forbade any conversation on the way, but when they were safely back in their room, he whispered:

"The stage is set at last, young 'un. We leave here to-morrow morning, and by to-morrow night the die will be cast. I only hope that Von Wadstein is in residence. It would be unfortunate if he were not there when we draw the net."

"Do you really think we shall sweep them in, guv'nor?"

"I don't think at all —I know. I tell you, Tinker, I am going to get

Augustus Keever before this time to-morrow night, and in the same drag I am going to gather in whomsoever else is there. Now let us get back to bed."

JUST about the time when Sexton Blake and Tinker were holding their secret confab with the French detective in the shadow of the wood outside Uxes, another consultation, even more secret if possible, was taking place in a room at the mansion belonging to Prince von Wadstein —the same which Blake was hearing about at that moment.

The parties to this conversation consisted only of two persons, and that it was of a most confidential nature was evident from the setting of the scene.

The room was a small boudoir, furnished in the heavy German style of the first Frederick, which adjoined the bedroom occupied by Marie, Nirvana's sister. There was sufficient chill in the air for her to have given orders for a fire to be lighted, and she was now seated before the blaze in silk neglige, while close to her was Philippe the Fox. Both were smoking, and when they spoke it was in whispers.

It was Marie's rendezvous, and for upwards of half an hour she had been leading up to the point, she had to make. She knew her man to the fifth degree, but what she had to propose that night was something of a nature which she had never before suggested and she knew that, despite her almost complete influence over him, he would present difficulties on this occasion, if for no other reason than that he had always had a sneaking regard for Nirvana.

And Marie's utterly soulless mind had evolved a plot that was bound to make even the Fox flinch. Her only hope of gaining his consent was to arrange things so it should be her hand to perform what action was necessary —for him to hold but a watching brief, so to say.

And even then the Fox was showing signs of jibbing.

"But don't you realise what a devil of a risk it means?" he asked, when he finally sensed what Marie was driving at. "You know I am no fool, and am as willing to take a chance as anyone. But I don't see what we are to gain by taking such a step as this. We have hit most of the 'high spots' in our partnership, Marie, but we have never gone quite as far as this. I have killed my man it is true, but I have never committed a murder, and you can't deny that this plan of yours would mean that and nothing else.

"As for the rest of it, I am game if you can show me how it is to be brought off. Don't forget that we are surrounded by people who are Von Wadstein's servants. They are just so many spies. And Keever isn't going to let us get away with that if he can help it. And, getting back to the other, what is the advantage in doing to Nirvana and the other one what you suggest doing?"

Marie made an impatient gesture.

"I am not going into detail about Nirvana," she said tensely, and her eyes glittered with hatred of her sister. "You know how I feel about her; you know what atrocious luck has dogged us ever since she first broke away. Time and again she has betrayed us, and you know it!

"Don't worry about Von Wadstein. He, at least, is a man —not frightened of making a bold stroke, like you and Keever. He would have been well pleased if Nirvana had remained in that dungeon in Venice; and you can take it from me that he would approve what I suggest about her, and that Cartier woman who has chosen to thrust herself into our affairs. If you do your part and leave the rest to me it will come off all right."

"How would you do it?" asked the Fox weakening. And Marie knew she had him.

"The whole thing fits in together," she whispered, drawing even closer. "Let Von Wadstein keep what Keever has already sent him. We don't need that. But we know that Keever brought with him not less than a million pounds in American bank-notes which he has been collecting for months as he realised on his various holdings. Well, we haven't done so badly, but why should we be such fools as to let Keever get away with the bulk of it?

"You will find that Von Wadstein will have little use for Keever now that he cannot go back to England. He was only useful as a power there. And with Keever out of the way there is no reason why we shouldn't work direct with Von Wadstein.

"We are not bound by the limits of any country. I have reason to believe that Von Wadstein intends extending his activities to America; we could handle that for him. What I propose is just what the prince would approve of.

"Now for the details. I took you out to the small island in the lake this afternoon because I wanted you to see it before I spoke to you about my plan. You had a good look at the stone building on it?"

"Of course."

"Well, that is something else besides being a prison for Nirvana and her companion. The main wing is Von Wadstein's laboratory. I took the trouble to cultivate him in Venice, and he told me about it. There are enough chemicals and explosives there to blow the whole place sky-high. And I have found out how it can be done. Now do you see my plan?"

"I can see what would happen to Nirvana and the other girl if it was blown up while they were in it," grunted the Fox.

"Exactly! Well, Keever won't refuse to go across in order to speak with Nirvana. He is crazier than ever about her, and will not suspect anything.

"My plan is that to-morrow evening, if Von Wadstein hasn't returned, we shall take the boat and go for a row on the lake after dinner. Keever will come —you can leave him to me. I shall then get him on to the island and into the building to talk with Nirvana. I can tell him that Nirvana wants to see him.

"Then, when he is inside, I lock the door and get into the laboratory. Give me five minutes there and I shall have things fixed so the whole place will blow to smithereens.

"You will be waiting in the boat ready to take me off when I come running. That is all there will be for you to do. And not only are all three of those persons wiped out once and for all, but every stiver of Keever's boodle is ours as well. Now Philippe, what about it?"

As she finished speaking, Marie slipped to her knees and put up her arms. Her head lifted, her eyes, hard no longer, but soft and inviting, gazed into Philippe's. He fought for a few moments against the lure of her; then suddenly, fiercely, he caught her to him.

"All right you —devil," he whispered. "I'll do it! I'll go the limit for you!"

And thus was cold-blooded murder planned by that precious pair.

THE NINTH CHAPTER.

Safety and Retribution.

SEXTON BLAKE and Tinker left the inn at Uxes at mid-morning of the day following their secret interview with Roger.

They took a leisurely way through the village, each carrying a paper parcel in which had been wrapped a cold lunch. The wood, which was their objective, was a perfectly natural spot to choose to rest and eat. And, sharp to the minute, came the French detective.

With him, as promised, he brought the plan of the Wadstein estate which his colleague, Jules, had prepared. It was but a rough affair, but it served Blake's purpose. In a quarter of an hour he had learned what he needed about the general plan of the estate and, with it on his knees, he listened to Roger's latest report.

"All is not so smooth as it should be, m'sieu. Figurez-vous! This island here which m'sieu can see marked in the centre of the little lake —Jules informs me that he has been able to discover its purpose. It is a private laboratory used by Prince von Wadstein. The prince is not at the mansion at present; so much is Jules certain of. And two of the demoiselles who were in the party remain all the time in this island house."

Blake shot a glance at Tinker.

"That means Yvonne and Nirvana," he muttered. "Go on, Roger!"

"The others remain in the mansion, m'sieu. The big man is almost always alone; the other two —Philippe the Fox, of our knowledge, and the woman —walk much together in the grounds and talk in confidential way. Also, early this morning they visited the island; but Jules dared not go close enough to see whether they entered the stone building, there or not. That is all, m'sieu."

"And a most helpful report it is, Roger. With this plan and what you have told me I am now ready to act."

"When, m'sieu?"

"To-night. Can you have the others on hand?"

"Of a surety, m'sieu."

"The chief problem is how to cross the river without being detected by the guards on the German side."

"I have had that in mind, m'sieu. I know of a spot, but it will be necessary to swim."

"That is a small difficulty to surmount. And, of course, we shall have to get back. What about the guards on this side?"

"They present no difficulty, m'sieu."

"Good! I leave those details to you, Roger. And we shall need two large saloon-cars. Can you arrange for them?"

"As many as m'sieu desires. Which way is it that we go after, m'sieu?"

"I have been pondering on that, Roger. I think it would be best to make a dash right through Luxembourg and into Belgium. But if you have another suggestion —"

"No, m'sieu; I should take that way, I think."

"Very well. And now about a place for me and my assistant to lie in hiding until nightfall. It will be clear, with stars, from the look of the weather —and, luckily, no moon."

"If m'sieu pleases I think it would be best to go into hiding close to the estate. It is very quiet there, and the thick woods offer many spots. If m'sieu is ready I shall take him along now."

So, under Roger's guidance, Blake and Tinker travelled several more kilometres until they came to a stretch of ill-kept woods on the same side of the river. It was quiet, apparently deserted country, and in the still hours of the afternoon it was easy enough to strip, and, with their clothes in a bundle on their heads, to swim across. They took cover in the woods of which Roger had spoken, and then there was nothing to do but to lie doggo and wait for night.

It was as close as may be to nine o'clock when Blake and Tinker came out on the edge of the private lake to which Roger had guided them. In a clump of trees there they came upon Jules and the other three agents who had been working along the Rhine valley. One at a time they had managed to reach the rendezvous without being spotted, and now each man was armed and ripe for whatever might break.

The island and stone building on it was only visible as a blur on the lake —all but one window, from which a light shone. From what Roger had told him Blake knew it to be roughly a hundred yards from the shore —not much to swim if a boat was not procurable.

But it seemed that the indefatigable Jules had made good use of his afternoon, for he assured Blake that he had found a flat-bottomed punt among some reeds at the other side of the lake, and when dusk had fallen had succeeded in getting it considerably nearer the rendezvous.

"But the others from the mansion went out to the island about an hour ago. m'sieu," he whispered. "I have not seen them return, but it is possible that they may have done so from the other side of the island."

"We will find the punt and go out, in any event," returned Blake, who had long ago made up his mind that Yvonne and Nirvana were being kept prisoners on the island until Von Wadstein should return.

His plans had been laid on the assumption that Von Wadstein would be there with the others, and, further, that all would be residing in the mansion, thus making it possible to concentrate his attack on one point.

Blake gave Roger brief instructions, telling him what he proposed doing, and warning him to keep a sharp look-out with the other three men while Jules accompanied him and Tinker to the island. The Frenchman had just indicated that he could be depended on, when Blake felt a sharp tug at his sleeve, and, turning, saw Tinker pointing across the lake.

"Look, guv'nor —look! The lower part of the building seems to be afire."

Blake gave one startled glance, then he turned as if to catch hold of Jules, when he stopped short. A woman's voice reached them across the narrow span of water as clearly as if she were close beside them. She was speaking in quite an ordinary tone; but sound travels clearly across still water, and the sinister mockery of it was far more impressive than if she had shouted her words.

"You may as well know now that the place is well alight," they heard. "Keever can tell you that the place is stacked with enough chemicals and explosives to blow the whole building to pieces. You won't have long to wait. We have seen to that. And when monseigneur returns we shall have a sad tale to tell him.

"You will not have much time left for love-making, Keever, so you had better make the most of it. As for you, Nirvana, you were well warned not to cross my will. And you, who are known as Mademoiselle Yvonne, you will be able to realise that I brook no interference from busybodies of your sort. While the other two are love-making you may pray for aid from your wonderful Sexton Blake —but you will pray in vain.

"Au revoir! We shall take good care of your property, Keever. Pull away, Philippe; the place will be a furnace soon, and when it goes it will go sky-high!"

As the terrible words died away a low laugh followed; then the faint splash of oars, as apparently the Fox obeyed her command.

Sexton Blake waited for no more. Throwing off his coat, he paused just long enough to pour out a swift explanation in French of the terrible devilry that was afoot —just that, and to rap:

"Get your men spread out, Roger! You, Jules, remain here now! Find that boat somehow and keep it under cover of your weapons. My assistant and I will swim for the island; if the boat tries to head us off, shoot —and shoot to kill those murderers!"

Then Blake dashed into the water, with Tinker close beside him. Shoulder to shoulder they struck out towards the island, their eyes on the red glow which was now spreading with terrific rapidity.

Stacked with enough chemicals and explosives to blow the whole building to pieces! That was what Marie had said —for they had recognised her voice plainly enough —and Sexton Blake knew only too well what destruction even a moderate laboratory explosion could cause. It was appalling to think what would happen if they were too late.

And above that inferno were Yvonne and Nirvana, not to mention Augustus Keever. Just what he was doing there, or why Marie and Philippe the Fox had "double-crossed" him, Blake didn't know, but he could make a pretty good guess.

Nor did it occur to either him or Tinker for a single moment that if the place was to go up, as seemed threatened, they too, would be wiped out of existence with it. Only one thought filled their minds — to rescue Yvonne and Nirvana. Keever, too, they thought of, but, in truth, only incidentally.

Two-thirds of the distance had been covered when they were simultaneously aware that a boat was making towards them.

Then a wild pandemonium broke loose. From the shore they could hear Roger shouting at the top of his lungs. Followed cries from the boat as Marie shrieked orders to unseen persons.

Then came the rapid rat-tat-tat of shooting. Bullets began to plomp into the water just ahead of them.

At another part of the shore lights sprang up as Wadstein's servants came in response to Marie's cries, but Roger and some at least of his companions were concentrating on the boat which threatened Blake and Tinker, for it sheered off, and, with a thin barrage ahead of them, Blake and Tinker made a final dash for the shore of the island.

For yards around the water was now lighted up by the glare of the flames in the lower part of the building. As they staggered through the shallow water and mud they could see three heads at a window high overhead. Pausing in their forward progress, Blake called:

"It is Blake and Tinker. There is no time to lose. Do you know how many doors there are to get through?"

There was a sharp cry of hope in a voice which Tinker knew was Nirvana's, but it was Yvonne who answered, her words trembling with emotion as she realised how Sexton Blake had come to her.

"There is the staircase door at the bottom," she called, trying to keep her voice on a level register, "and one at the top. This one is bolted on the outside, but I think among us we can break it open. The other is very heavy and I don't know how you will manage it."

"We'll manage it," called back Blake. "You three get busy at once. Is that you, Keever?"

"Yes," came a low reply which it was difficult to recognise as the voice of the arrogant financier.

"Then if you ever used your weight, use it now," responded Blake curtly. "The whole place is alight —there is no time now to try and extinguish the fire —make haste —"

"We go now," Yvonne called. "And if we are too late you will know —"

"Try hard, please," added Nirvana bravely, and at those words Tinker couldn't have spoken no matter how hard he tried.

But there was no time now for anything but to break a way in — if possible.

The battle between Roger with the other four, and Von Wadstein's servants was now at its height. What had become of Marie and the Fox they didn't know. Nor were they concerned just then.

They raced round the corner of the building and each gave a gasp of horror as they saw, through a heat-smashed window, the raging inferno within. It seemed utterly hopeless to try and force the door which led to the staircase.

But those two were driven by an impelling urge, and it was a pair of maniacs that attacked the heavy door which held the way to freedom for those above.

Crash! Crash! Crash!

Time after time they hurled themselves bodily at the thick wood; time after time they gripped each other so as to combine every atom of strength. From the smashed window terrible blasts of smoke and flame sought them.

Crash! Crash-s-s-s-sh!

That last effort ended in a long, rending, tearing sound of splintering wood. The next drive carried them clean through to the lobby within.

They knew that not many minutes could possibly elapse now before the explosion came. When it did, they were aware, from what they had seen, that everything on that island would simply vanish from material existence.

Lurching in the smoke-filled entry, they stared up the stairs. Would Keever and the two girls be able to break open the upper door. Or would they be able to get there in time to tear it open from their side?

And then, through the smoke, they saw a figure. Blake rushed forward just in time to catch Yvonne, who was almost fainting from smoke. Tinker tore past him, and came staggering down a moment later bearing Nirvana close to him. After the lad, on the point of suffocation, came Augustus Keever.

Not one of the five has a clear recollection of how they got out of the building and to the edge of the water. Blake paused only long enough to catch Keever by the shoulder with a free hand and urge him to the edge.

"Can you swim?" he demanded sharply.

"Y-e-s," came the choking reply.

"Then, if you want to live, swim now. And if we can get clear, heaven help you if you try to escape! Come on, Tinker!"

With that Blake took the water, Tinker following close, and Keever mechanically following. Once away from the shore, both the girls revived sufficiently to make an effort for themselves,

With every yard they covered Blake breathed easier. Half the distance —two-thirds —the shore was plainly visible now through the gloom, and the roar and flash of weapons told him that his men were still holding their ground.

Only twenty yards —ah, his foot had touched mud bottom —a

few strokes and a few strides, and then —

BOOM! BO-O-OM! BO-O-OM!

Three appalling explosions seemed to rend the whole universe about them, so completely did it dominate everything else. The whole lake became light as day for the space of perhaps five seconds, while the little party was hurled flat under the terrific concussion which beat on to water and shore. Then the whole earth seemed to descend upon them as the debris rained in every direction.

Somehow Sexton Blake gained his feet, and sought for Yvonne. He found her, sobbing hysterically from the shock. He saw Tinker lurching ashore with an unconscious Nirvana in his arms; and, quite dazed. Augustus Keever was allowing himself to be led by Roger, who appeared to have escaped any serious effects of the explosion.

They traversed the woods as in a nightmare; they reached the river at last, and there, with immediate pursuit a thing not to be worried about, Blake was only too glad to-resign himself and his charges to Roger and his fellows.

The crossing was made in safety; then another staggering progress to the two waiting cars; and, after that, a rush through the cool night, dashing recklessly across half the breadth of Luxembourg, and past gaping frontier guards into Belgium.

IT was a great feat, no matter how one might look at it.

It was a magnificent victory of courage that was an epic. It was that which created a bond between rescuers and rescued which nothing would, or could wipe out. It was one of the greatest feats of Sexton Blake's career, for out of that inferno of gas and smoke and flame he had brought his man.

The events of that terrible night made a deep impression on Augustus Keever. When Blake inquired curtly, after the formal arrest, if he intended to fight extradition to England, Keever shook his head.

"No. I'll go back without trouble. I'll face the music and do what I can to straighten up the muddle. I can command enough money yet to repay everyone who bought forged Polonian bonds.

He kept his promise, and while the trial was one of the most sensational held in London for many years, Augustus Keever would have received a much longer term than the seven years' penal servitude which was passed, had Sexton Blake chosen to expose more of his knowledge of Keever's career.

But that night at the island had not left Blake untouched, and he knew from Yvonne that in the critical moments when they expected the place to be blown to pieces Keever had displayed consideration and chivalry.

For that Sexton Blake forgave him much.

They heard nothing definite as to what had become of Marie and Philippe the Fox. Nor did they know what attitude Von Wadstein took when he learned of the events which had occurred during his absence. But Blake had no doubt that Marie would be able to devise a tale that would serve her purpose. And in that he was right, as he was to learn.

The stage was already being set for the biggest battle of all; the fate which ruled Sexton Blake and Prince von Wadstein was again juggling with their planets.

Even then was the appointed hour at hand —and Sexton Blake was ready.

THE END.
[24600 WORDS]

THREE SPLENDID
PRESENTATION PLATES
IN FULL COLOUR!

SIXPENNY MAGAZINES
Ask your newsagent for one of These
*Sixpenny Magazines are back again. Four of the best known,
THE PREMIER MAGAZINE (hitherto 1s.) and THE RED, THE
MERRY, and THE VIOLET Magazines (hitherto 7d. each) are all on
sale now at 6d. each.*

*A new Magazine, THE ALL-STORY, has just been published also
at 6d.*

*In every case the quality and quantity of the contents of these
magazines makes them altogether exceptional value for money. Make
a note of the names! Ask for them at your newsagent's or bookstall.
Better magazine value for 6d. is unobtainable.*

Printed and published every Thursday by the Proprietors, The
Amalgamated Press (1922), Ltd., The Fleetway House, Farringdon
Street, London, E.C.4. Advertisement offices: The Fleetway House,
Farringdon Street, London, E.C.4. Registered for transmission by
Canadian Magazine Post. Subscription rates: Inland and Abroad, 11s.
per annum; 5s. 6d. for six months. Sole agents for South Africa: The
Central News Agency, Ltd. Sole agents for Australia and New
Zealand; Messrs. Gordon & Gotch, Ltd; and for Canada, The Imperial
News Co., Ltd. (Canada).— Saturday, October 30th, 1926.

the **UNION JACK**
—correct in every detail

SOMETHING IMPORTANT!
The most frequent request of "U.J." readers in asking for a special treat is for a coloured plate on notable occasions.

Those many requests have not been ignored. The notable occasion will soon be here, and —we are not presenting merely one special picture in full colours, but THREE special pictures!

They will be presented with every copy of the "U. J." for three consecutive weeks, beginning with the copy on sale on November 11th, which is Armistice Day.

That is the notable occasion, and it is one which will be fittingly celebrated for U. J. readers in this splendid three-week presentation. The trio of pictures records the most momentous event in our times — the Armistice as it came to the rejoicing throngs in the Empire's capital; to the soldiers who re-entered Mons after the fighting; and to the sailors escorting the beaten German Fleet to its last anchorage.

You will have no idea of how good these plates ready are till you see them for yourself. This announcement is merely a hint to you not to neglect getting your regular copy. Next week fuller details will be given; next week also will appear the next Nirvana story – The last of the present series of episodes, which, of course you must not miss, entitled:
"A MYSTERY OF THE MOUNTAINS!"

Regular readers must certainly get next Thursday's issue and discover more about our magnificent colour-plates —THREE of them.

A Mystery in the Mountains *is available in a Stillwoods Edition. . . /drf*

—correct in every detail

BING
ELECTRIC TRAINS

Bing Engines are perfectly constructed
miniatures built by engineers. You can
buy a whole system or build one by
buying separately Engines, Rolling
Stock, Tracks, Signals, Tunnels, Stations, etc. Call to-day at your nearest
toy shop and ask for your copy of the
complete Bing Catalogue of models. In
addition to trains it illustrates Bing
Magic Lanterns and Cinemas, Tractors,
Stationary Engines, Dynamo Plants,
Steam Rollers, etc., etc. In case of
difficulty write to address below.

*Look for this Brand
Mark on all metal toys.*

Send for free booklet

to
**Bing Advertising Department 8,
Lincoln House, High Holborn, London, W.C. 1.**

70

BING
ELECTRIC TRAINS

Bing Engines are perfectly constructed miniatures built by engineers. You can buy a whole system or build one by buying separately Engines, Rolling Stock, Tracks, Signals, Tunnels, Stations, etc. Call to-day at your nearest toy shop and ask for your copy of the complete Bing Catalogue of models. In addition to trains it illustrates Bing Magic Lanterns and Cinemas, Tractors, Stationary Engines, Dynamo Plants, Steam Rollers, etc., etc. In case of difficulty write to address below.

**to
Bing Advertising Department 8,
Lincoln House, High Holborn, London, W.C. 1.**

www.ingramcontent.com/pod-product-compliance
Lightning Source LLC
Chambersburg PA
CBHW031901170626
46807CB00004B/1833